PRAISE FOR "THE UNLIVED LIVES OF RAYMOND QUINN"

Many thanks to the readers who took the time to review *The Unlived Lives of Raymond Quinn*, the first book in the "Unlived Lives" series.

"Perfect for anyone who likes a bit of everything—philosophy, adventure, and a good, page-turning plot. One of my top books for 2024…"

———

"Very interesting and intriguing delve into alternative lives emanating from one young man's tragic demise during the war in Vietnam."

———

"This is an excellent story to read about life decisions, second chances and one that will have you thinking about your own life choices."

———

"The author explores complex themes including life and death, the afterlife, and the rippling consequences of our decisions."

———

"Thought-provoking read that has inspired a litany of 'what if's' relative to this reviewer's own life. Enjoyed this well-written book very much."

———

"It presents a hauntingly reflective journey of life, memory, and fate. Thought-provoking twists will keep your attention as layers of Raymond's life unfold."

———

"A good read for fans of science fiction and history or anyone who has ever wondered about the existence of parallel universes."

———

"What began as an apparent thriller/mystery as to how the protagonist found himself in his present situation, evolved into a narrative spanning 50 years involving multiple characters, countries, and conflicts."

———

"If you're drawn to psychological depth, mystery, and the exploration of the human condition, this book is for you."

———

"If you like parallel universe stories like Blake Crouch's 'Dark Matter,' you need to meet Raymond Quinn. "

Paperback: 979-8-9909986-2-9

Ebook: 979-8-9909986-3-6

Audiobook available on Audible.

CREDITS

Cover design: Paula L. Johnson Creative Services

Cover image: murat4art / iStock

Page design: Vellum

Dog tag art: Kyle Matthies

Author jacket photo: Skye Moorhead

Audiobook narration: JT Farrell

WilliamMatthies.com

Published by William Matthies

THE UNLIVED LIVES OF SHELLY BENNETT

BENNETT

UNLIVED LIVES · BOOK 2

WILLIAM MATTHIES

"Don't be afraid of death;
be afraid of an unlived life."

Natalie Babbitt from *Tuck Everlasting*

PROLOGUE

Shelly!

What? Who is this?

I am you!

Me? Where am I?

On your way to where you chose to be. You killed yourself. Your mortal life has ended. I will help you determine the fate of your immortal soul.

I killed myself? I wouldn't do that; there must be a mistake.

That was your fatal mistake.

You ended your mortal life, but you can choose what your immortal existence will be. A future where your soul will exist in a universe parallel to the one in which you lived your mortal life.

Choose carefully; what you choose is for eternity.

CHAPTER
ONE

My mortal life ended because I committed suicide? I can now choose my immortal life. That can't be, that has to be a dream. But I will commit suicide if I have to remain in this God-forsaken country much longer. I will get out one way or another.

Almost sure she was dreaming, a part of Shelly suspected otherwise. Something about her life was very different in ways she hadn't anticipated. Now, she could think of nothing else.

A dream, a very bad dream, because I want to leave Zimbabwe as soon as possible. That's all it was. But still... What am I missing? I need to know something else, something about my dream. What is it? I am stuck in a country whose government I detest. Most countries I might be interested in won't even accept applications from Zimbabwean citizens. Why bother trying? And those that do aren't any better than where I am now. Maybe South Africa? It's open to those with university degrees, which might help its economy. Whether or not that would include me, I don't know.

The border between the two countries is highly porous, with large numbers of Zimbabwean citizens crossing illegally. Shelly thought about becoming one of them but decided against it. Her long-term happiness required her to immigrate legally.

She had completed the required paperwork and hand-delivered her application to the South African consulate in Harare over a year ago. No word regarding her status until the mail arrived this afternoon, including an envelope bearing the South African government return address. She desperately wanted to open it, telling herself she would move there if approved, while knowing that wasn't what she wanted to do. South Africa was only an option if she could find no other alternative, and to this point, there were none she would consider.

Shelly stood in her living room, envelope in hand, staring at the South African Office of Immigration return address.

There's only one way to find out.

She tore open the envelope and removed a one-page response to her immigration application.

17 March 1975

Re: Applicant, Miss Shelly Bennett

Please be advised that your request to immigrate to South Africa, dated 9 February 1974, has been denied. You do not meet South Africa's minimum requirements for permanent residency.

If you feel this decision is incorrect, you may visit the South African consulate office nearest you to obtain more information regarding the reasons for rejecting your application. If at that time you wish to do so, you may pay the review request fee and complete the necessary forms, providing whatever additional information you feel may impact the decision. A second review will be initiated, and you will be notified of the results when that report becomes available.

Thank you for your interest in immigrating to South Africa.

Regards,

Reginald Goutily

Assistant Administration Manager

South African Office of Immigration

Shelly let the letter and envelope fall to the floor. She looked out the window of her Sinoia Street apartment toward the inner city rail station a block away. Her private space where she often retreated when life outside became too difficult. Smaller than a Western studio apartment, it hadn't bothered her before. Now, it suddenly felt as though the walls were closing in on her. She didn't know what she would do, but she did have a plan if all else failed.

Shelly had a recurring dream, one that increasingly became real the more she found life in Zimbabwe intolerable. In this dream, she left

Zimbabwe to travel. She had no detailed plan of where she would go, no schedule, and her only limit was how long she could stay away before running out of money.

But there was more to it than that.

If I can't find a country that will accept me permanently, why not travel as a tourist? I've dreamed of doing that. I can visit other places I might like to live. Who knows, I might find some way to stay. Antigua would be a good place to start. At least it was in my dream.

Still staring out the window, Shelly's mind focused on the dream, her time in Antigua, and…

There was someone with me. Why can't I recall who? I know it's just a dream, and there's more I can't remember than that I can. There was something about whoever that was that set them apart from all others. That person was special. I can't stand not knowing. I must remember!

Suddenly very tired, Shelly lay back on the sofa, quickly falling asleep, her last conscious thoughts hoping to dream again about Antigua.

CHAPTER
TWO

YOU CAN REMEMBER. CONCENTRATE, THINK ABOUT WHAT YOU DID WITH THIS person whose name you cannot recall. You will find what you are looking for.

I do remember. We were together on a beach. We had dinner together. A young man, or boy, we were both young. He wanted me to go somewhere with him. Where? Did we go? What was his name? What little I remember is real enough; he must be, too.

You know, Shelly, only you could know. You also know what you will do if you choose not to remember. Is that what you want? This is about much more than your unhappy life in Zimbabwe. You have options, but you are focusing on only one. The wrong one. Continue doing that, and there is no turning back. Your life as you know it will end. There will be a continuance, but not as you hope. Your mortal life over, your immortal life will begin, one you did not choose.

————

Shelly awoke suddenly, quickly sitting upright, staring into the distance, seeing nothing. Her dream replaced by conversation, but with whom she couldn't say.

A conversation? With myself? It had to be. Maybe a dream, a premonition. I don't know. I'm not talking with anyone other than myself. So...what am I telling myself to do? I know what I'm thinking, is that what I want?

Shelly spent the rest of the day and into the night thinking only about her dream. She questioned her thoughts, wondering if they meant something important or just something she dreamed. Either way, it didn't matter.

There's no other place I'd want to live. No point moving somewhere that's no better than here. If only life could be as I dream it, traveling to find an alternative life.

That thought left her feeling empty.

There was someone in my dream, a young man on a beach. I have good feelings about him, although I can't recall his face or even his name. I can't stand it! I know what to do, and now is the time. I may be dreaming. I don't know. I don't care. I will end this insanity now!

Shelly got up from the couch and walked to the desk beside her bed. Opening the drawer, she took out a shoebox, carefully placing it on the desk, the lid beside it. She paused, looking at the contents of the box as she had many times before.

But I am certain now this is what I must do. This is the solution I've been seeking.

Shelly took the gun out of the box, put it to her forehead, and pulled the trigger.

CHAPTER
THREE

I won't ask you to explain your choice; it was yours to make. You ended your mortal life because you saw no alternatives to an existence you were convinced you could no longer tolerate. There are consequences for you having done so. That was your choice, but you have impacted an infinite number of people, both living and those who would have lived had you not killed yourself.

If this does not matter to you, you will exist in a universe separate and parallel to the one in which you lived your mortal life. Just one of an infinite number of alternatives you would have lived had you made different choices. What that is, and what it will become, is not entirely yours to decide. You forfeited that right when you chose to end your mortal life. However, you are one of an infinitesimally small number of people who are allowed to affect their immortal souls' existence. Do you understand?

Not all of it, but you will tell me that no longer matters. I am not in control of my immortal destiny. Is that it?

Essentially, yes, but what you decide now will determine what that destiny will be. You don't need to understand. Listen carefully to what I tell you.

Shelly was listening more than she had ever listened to anything as a mortal. Her mind, no longer troubled by her life in Zimbabwe, she considered where she would rather live if she could move elsewhere.

She found peace in her mortal death, curious about her immortal future.

You decided to kill yourself. Your dreams taunted you regarding an alternative life. You can now reconsider some of those decisions. To do that, you must visit some of the alternative lives you would have lived had you chosen differently in your mortal life, only one of which will give you answers to questions you do not know to ask. That choice is yours.

Still struggling to make sense of what was happening, Shelly began to understand her situation.

You do not know where you are, but do you know where you were?

Zimbabwe! Yes, I do, am I still there?

Your lifeless, mortal body is your soul is not. Your body no longer matters; focus only on your soul, choosing what will become of it.

How do I choose? What am I choosing?

You have some control over your immortal fate. You put the gun to your head, you pulled the trigger. At that moment, your mortal life ended. You are now at a crossroads between your mortal and immortal lives. The one in which you lived and died, parallel to the one you must now live for eternity. The time has come, Shelly. What do you choose?

My decision. It is no longer about my mortality. I've ended that. It is about my immortality. I have one question to ask before I choose. Is that acceptable?

Yes.

Does what I choose have anything to do with Raymond Quinn?

You will know, depending on which unlived lives you choose to visit. You will know when it is time to leave a place, person, or situation. Do not minimize the importance of what you choose. Do not put off changing something you know is wrong. Doing so is a decision, the consequences of which will end your ability to choose your immortal life.

CHAPTER
FOUR

SHELLY'S IMMIGRATION APPLICATION TO SOUTH AFRICA REJECTED, AND with no prospects for any other countries of interest to her, she decided to travel on tourist visas.

She looked forward to her first international stop, Caracas, Venezuela, but had not contemplated how difficult getting there would be. No direct flights between Zimbabwe and Venezuela; the three-stop trip would take thirty-plus hours of flight and layover time. She had to watch how much she spent, opting for the least expensive itinerary, which was also the longest travel time.

Now, on the final segment, exhausted, unable to sleep as much as she had planned to, Shelly second-guessed her choice for a first destination.

This wouldn't have been as bad if I had stayed in a hotel in Madrid instead of spending the night at the airport. I saved the cost of a room, but it's taking an extra day of my time to travel. I hope this is worth the time, money, and effort.

———

Once off the plane, too exhausted to feel nervous, Shelly handed her passport and arrival card to the immigration officer at Simón Bolívar

International Airport. He accepted them, carefully studying her and her passport photo.

"¿Dónde te alojarás mientras estés en Venezuela?"

"Sorry, I don't understand?"

The officer repeated the question in English, sounding slightly perturbed.

"I asked where you will be staying while in Venezuela. Your arrival card says you are staying at a hostel. We must have the name and address."

"I apologize. I was so tired on the flight, I overlooked that. I have it here," she said, reaching into her bag for her Venezuela trip information.

"Please hurry, many people are waiting. You should have completed the required information before getting in line."

Shelly found the reservation card and held it out for the officer.

"You must complete the information on the card. I cannot do it for you. Please show me your flight information departing Venezuela."

Shelly did as he said, thinking that all immigration officials sound so much alike—curt, bordering on angry.

But I suppose I would be, too, if all I did all day was deal with people who hadn't properly followed directions.

"I see you have a thirty-day visa, and your departure flight is three weeks from today. You should have been informed before you left your country that, due to special circumstances, Venezuela has temporarily shortened your visa class to a maximum of fourteen days. You must rebook your departure no later than fourteen days from today. An officer will visit you at the hostel address you provide to verify that you have done so. Make sure that you do."

The officer handed Shelly's travel papers back to her, including her passport with the approved entry stamp. Having collected her luggage and cleared customs, she looked for the cheapest way to get to Caracas from the airport. She assumed it was close by, but soon learned otherwise.

The quickest way would be by taxi, not an option for Shelly given the cost. Instead, she would take a local bus from the domestic terminal, more than doubling the trip time for a fraction of what a taxi would cost. She found the city bus terminal, paid the fare, and boarded the bus for the approximate one-hour ride to Caracas.

What 'special circumstances' would cause Venezuela to reduce how much time I can stay? Does this apply only to me or everyone arriving today? I suppose one week, more or less, won't matter much. And if all Venezuelans are as abrupt as the officer, I may decide to leave even sooner.

Finally, in Venezuela, on the bus, she relaxed and took in the sights. The bus route was up a steep, winding road lined with shacks close together on both sides. The people living in them appeared very poor, the children barefoot and dirty.

Looking out the window as the bus slowly made its way toward the city center, Shelly thought that what she had seen so far was not all that different from Salisbury.

I'm not sure I need to be here at all if this is all there is.

The bus pulled into an outdoor terminal where passengers departed and collected their luggage, sheltered under a large overhead tarp meant to protect those below from the weather. Shelly looked up to see that it was full of holes, some larger than a melon, many of her fellow passengers were carrying.

Good that it's not raining. If it were, we'd be getting soaked. I'm the only one who does not appear to be a local. The only one with a suitcase. All the others are carrying large cotton bags. I suppose filled with what they bought in the open seaside market, Catia La Mar, adjacent to the airport.

A short walk later, she was at her hostel, El Sofá Caracas, and checked into her shared room.

CHAPTER
FIVE

Less than three days since I took the train from my apartment to Harare airport. So much has happened, so little sleep. All I want to do now is shower and go to bed. But is that what I should do? I only have so much time in Caracas, now a week less than I planned. And if I were to go to bed now, I'd probably not sleep tonight. No, I'll shower but not go to bed. I'll go out and get something to eat, forcing myself to stay up a while longer.

Her shower finished, Shelly was back in her room finishing unpacking when a young woman who appeared to be about her age entered.

"I assume you're my new roommate; the desk said you had arrived while I was out. My name is Caroline Peel, happy to meet you."

"Nice to meet you, Caroline. I'm Shelly Bennett."

"Our accents are similar, although not the same. Am I correct in assuming you are not from the UK, as I am?"

Shelly smiled, "No, I'm not, but I would have guessed you were when you spoke. I'm from Rhodesia or Zimbabwe, if I'm being correct."

"Southern Africa, isn't it? My, you have come a long way, haven't you?"

"It is, I have, and I may just fall asleep as we talk if I'm not careful."

"Oh, I apologize; of course, you'd be trashed after such a long trip. You probably want nothing more than to sleep."

"Not a problem. I did plan to sleep before showering, but the shower brought me around at least somewhat. And I'm questioning whether I'll be able to sleep tonight if I do go to bed now, even for a little while."

"Have you eaten? If not, you really should before sleeping. I mean, you should if you're at all hungry. The neighborhood is reasonably safe, but you don't want to be out late after dark."

"I am hungry, but not as much as I thought I would be after three days of travel, eating airport and airline food. Is there something close by you'd recommend? Nothing heavy, just enough to ensure it won't be hunger that keeps me awake."

"Better than recommending something, how about I take you to a place I think you'll enjoy? Alila Cantina."

"That would be wonderful since I have no idea where I would go. You know the place, I don't. Let me pay for both of us."

Caroline smiled, "I used to laugh when I would hear my mum and her old friends arguing over who would pay. We're too young for that, let's split the check, agreed?"

"Agreed, when would you like to go? How dressy should I be? I can be ready in 15 minutes."

"Not dressy at all, as you can see, I'm not. Alila is nearby. They serve what Americans call 'comfort food.' Quite good, not expensive. Does that work for you?"

"Absolutely, and what better than American food for one of us still part of the empire, the other wishing she were too? I'll change clothes before I change my mind and go to bed. A good meal, good company, maybe a good pint, exactly what I need!"

CHAPTER
SIX

IT WAS A SHORT WALK FROM THE HOSTEL TO ALILA. SHELLY AND CAROLINE were quickly seated, pints of beer in front of them, getting more comfortable with each other by the minute. Close in age, both single, with similar backgrounds and education, adventurous enough to be traveling alone. All of that put Shelly at ease.

At one point, the conversation was mainly about how Shelly should spend her time and what she should see and do. Caroline had been in Caracas just short of two weeks, and told Shelly where she had been, what she thought was worth the time and money, as well as what wasn't. The conversation then turned to when each would leave and where they would go next.

"I've been here two weeks, day after tomorrow. What a great trip! It was so much fun, and now, having met you, I may extend my time a bit. What are your plans, Shelly?"

"Good question, I don't have a plan. I was working on one and then just decided to book myself here, figuring out the rest after. I leave for Antigua three weeks from today. However, the immigration officer made it clear: I need to leave in two weeks because of...what did he call it?" Shelly said, looking at a couple who had just entered the restaurant. "Special circumstances. He didn't say what they were, only that I needed to rebook my departure for two weeks from today, and an officer would come to the hostel to see that I did."

Hearing this, Caroline laughed.

"Oh, pish posh. I had a departure booked for ten days after I arrived. I was enjoying myself so much that I canceled it after a week, planning to rebook when I felt I'd seen and done enough. No one's come looking for me. I don't know what that's about, but I have met others who have been here longer than two weeks. If someone does come to check on you, just play dumb. Tell them you're sorry, you misunderstood the rule, you have a reservation to leave, and will do so in another week."

Shelly was surprised and pleased to hear this. She didn't know how she'd fill her time, but Caroline would likely have suggestions for her. The more the two talked, the more comfortable Shelly became, leaving her departure scheduled for three weeks. The two of them planned where Shelly would go and what she would do, some of it with Caroline, some of it on her own.

Dinner complete, they continued talking, drinking another three pints of Cerveza Polar. Caroline was okay with that, and Shelly would have been had she not just spent thirty-plus hours getting to Venezuela. Speaking slowly, her words slightly slurred, a side effect of not having slept, and the beer, she knew it was time to leave.

"This has been so much fun, Caroline! Thank you for inviting me and giving me ideas of what I should do. I want to stay here talking with you more, but if I do, if I have another Polar, you'd have to carry me to our room. Let me take care of the meal as a thank you before we head back."

"I enjoyed it too, and I look forward to us having more fun together for however much time we have left in Venezuela. But we did agree to split the check; let's stick to that."

"You're right. No harm trying, and I will make it up to you at some point."

The evening done, more so for Shelly than for Caroline, the two made their way back to the hostel.

"Go to bed, Shelly, you need to sleep. I'm not tired and am meeting up with friends. Let's have breakfast together."

"I will sleep. See you in the morning, Caroline."

CHAPTER
SEVEN

SHELLY SLEPT SOUNDLY UNTIL 5 AM WHEN HER JET LAG REVERSED, AND her mind decided it was time to wake up. The room was dark, but she thought she could make out the form of Caroline asleep under blankets across from her. She hadn't heard her come in and didn't want to disturb her until it was closer to breakfast at 7 AM. If she didn't go back to sleep, she would lie quietly, thinking about the day ahead. She would struggle later, but adjusting to multiple time zones would get easier over time.

What did Caroline suggest I do today? I remember. Within the city itself, Panteón Nacional houses the remains of prominent Venezuelans, including Simón Bolívar. And after, time permitting, the Teleferico cable car ride up to the view of Caracas, all the way to the sea below. She said she would enjoy revisiting both and would guide me there if I liked. Maybe she'll go with me. This is working out great! She knows where to go; I don't. We get along well, and I don't have to pay for a guide.

Shelly did not expect to go back to sleep, but did for another hour, waking as the sun was rising, throwing some light into the dark room.

Didn't expect to sleep more, glad I did. I feel better, even more so once I go to the bathroom. Hopefully, without waking Caroline, at least for a bit longer. If she doesn't wake up, I'll wake her in time for breakfast.

Shelly got up quietly, looking down at Caroline's bed before leaving the room on her way to the bathroom down the hall.

It's still too dark to be sure, but it doesn't look like there's even a body under those covers. And I don't see her head.

Shelly came back to the room, entering as quietly as possible, hoping Caroline would be awake. But with the increasing daylight in the room, she became more certain that whatever was under the covers was not large enough to be a person. Unsure, she moved to her bed, sitting on the side facing Caroline.

Do I wake her? It's still half an hour until breakfast, and I have no idea how late she was out last night. How do I know she even came back to the hostel?

Shelly thought about last night's dinner conversation, and after when Caroline said she wasn't tired enough to sleep and was going out to meet 'friends'.

Depending on who that was, maybe I'm not as important to her this morning as I thought I would be.

Unable to withstand the temptation any longer, Shelly crossed to Caroline's bed and lightly felt the blanket. Bolder now and every bit as curious, she slowly pulled it back far enough to see that Caroline was not there.

I hope she's ok. She said the neighborhood was safe enough, but it wasn't a good idea to be outside alone after dark. But that's precisely what she did, at least until she met with her friends or a friend. Well, I don't know anything for sure, so the best thing I can do is go on with the day, alone. I'll see her later this afternoon.

Shelly gathered her soap and shampoo, heading back to the bathroom to shower. Once that was done, she dressed and went to breakfast. The small dining area was filled with other guests she hadn't met.

I wonder if any of them know Caroline? One of them may know who she might be with or was with last night. But what do I do? Just start asking, 'Do any of you know Caroline? If so, do you know who she might have been with last night or where she is now? We're supposed to go sightseeing together today.' I can't do that.

Still concerned but seeing no alternative, Shelly decided to spend the day alone, visiting some of the activities Caroline suggested they do together.

Hopefully, she'll be back in our room when I return later this afternoon, apologizing for not going with me. Maybe even tell me what she did the rest of the night.

Her breakfast finished, Shelly left for the day, still curious about Caroline, but determined not to waste time waiting for her in the hostel. When she returned that afternoon, she found Caroline's side of the room was clean, the bed made, and no personal belongings in sight. She went down to the desk to see what they could tell her.

"Excuse me, do you know where my roommate, Caroline, is? I haven't seen her since dinner last night, and now her side of the room is clean, as though she's no longer here. I'm worried about her."

The desk clerk looked at the register before responding.

"I don't know where she is. This says she checked out last night around 8 PM. There's nothing about where she was going."

"Is there any indication she'll be back? Do you have any message for me? Did she seem upset?"

"There's nothing more about her in the register, no messages for you, and I wasn't here when she left."

Shelly thanked him and turned away from the desk, not sure what to do or think. She'd only met Caroline a little less than twenty-four hours ago, and while they got on well with each other, neither of them owed any explanation to the other about anything.

She wondered if she should contact the police.

But what would I say? 'My adult roommate, whom I just met, is missing. She was supposed to go sightseeing with me today. She didn't. Can you look for her?'

Shelly decided there was nothing she could do other than hope Caroline, or some word about or from her, would soon come.

CHAPTER
EIGHT

SHELLY ENJOYED HER TIME IN CARACAS AND THE SURROUNDING AREA despite there being no information regarding Caroline.

If she were in trouble and something had happened to her, the police would come to the hostel to interview everyone. None have, and no one in the hostel seems concerned.

She kept busy visiting some of the sites Caroline told her about, halfway expecting to see her at one or more of them.

She may yet walk up, apologizing for not leaving word where she was going, offering a plausible explanation for her absence. We could still finish the remainder of our time in Venezuela together.

That didn't happen, and now Shelly was beginning the third and final week of her stay.

Shortly after lunch, her fifteenth day in Caracas, she came back to the hostel planning to lie down to rest before heading out again. She walked into the lobby and saw a uniformed police officer looking at her, turning his head toward the clerk. The officer slightly tilted his head in Shelly's direction, the clerk nodded, and the officer immediately walked toward her.

"You are Shelly Bennett?"

"Yes, I am."

"You will please come with me."

"Where? I haven't done anything. Is this about Caroline?"

"Please, I insist you come with me; all your questions will be answered shortly."

Seeing no recourse, Shelly started toward the door with the officer next to her. She hadn't noticed his police car parked outside, another officer sitting in the back, when she returned from lunch. The first officer opened the door to the back seat, motioning for Shelly to get in. She did, and the three of them started for the police station.

Once there, Shelly was led into a room with a small table and two chairs. Told to sit, the officer asked if she would like a glass of water. She nodded, he left the room, and moments later, a third officer entered, holding a glass of water, which he placed on the table in front of Shelly. He sat down across from her, lit a cigarette, and offered her one. She shook her head, thanking him.

"I am Sergeant Balboa. You are Shelly Bennett, visiting Caracas from Zimbabwe, correct?"

"Yes, why am I here? I haven't done anything."

"Please be patient, I will ask the questions, and you will answer. You are a friend of a young woman named Caroline Peel, correct?"

"I met Caroline when I checked into the hostel where she was staying. We were placed in the same room. We had dinner together my first night, and made plans to sightsee together the next day. But she was not there when I got up. I asked about her, but no one could tell me anything other than she had checked out. I haven't seen her since, that's all I know. What has happened to her?"

"When you came through immigration at the airport, you were told your three-week visa was no longer valid, were you not?"

"Yes, I was, but…"

The officer cut her off.

"You were also told that you had to rebook your departure for two weeks, not three, from the date you entered the country. Is that also true?"

"Yes."

"Did you?"

Shelly could see that the officer knew the answers to the questions he was asking. She momentarily considered doing as Caroline told her to do, saying she didn't know how to rebook, got too busy sightseeing, or something like that. She decided not to; the officer would know she was lying.

"No."

"Why didn't you?"

"Caroline told me at dinner that first night that she met others who said they were told the same thing. No one came to verify when they would leave. She said she canceled her original departure reservation. It was now past two weeks, and she had no plans to reschedule because she was enjoying herself so much. She told me not to bother rebooking unless I wanted to leave after two weeks. I wanted to stay another week, leaving as I originally planned. Honestly, I didn't think anyone would check to see if I had changed my reservation. No one did, including the two officers who brought me here today."

The officer lit another cigarette with the butt of the first one, tamping it out in the ashtray. He took a long drag, blowing smoke through his nostrils, looking directly at Shelly—ten seconds, maybe more, passed with neither of them saying anything.

"Miss Bennett, you will be detained while we complete an investigation into the reason for your presence in Venezuela. It is in your best interest to fully cooperate with us, truthfully answering all our questions. Do you understand?"

Stunned, tears flooding her eyes, she struggled to speak.

"I am under arrest? Why? I haven't done anything, and I don't know anything more about Caroline than I've told you. Why are you doing this to me?"

"You are not under arrest, Miss Bennett; you are being detained. If, as you say, you have done nothing wrong, cooperate with us, tell the truth, and you will be released. Please wait here; a matron will come to you shortly. She will search you, providing you with the clothes you must wear while you are here. Goodbye for now, we will talk again later."

CHAPTER
NINE

YOU WILL KNOW WHEN IT IS TIME TO LEAVE A PLACE, PERSON, OR SITUATION.
Do you recall thinking that?

I do, but I don't know what it means.

You have visited one of your unlived lives based on the choices you made.
You do not know the outcome of that decision. How do you feel about what
you do know?

The police in Caracas, Venezuela, are holding me. I don't know why. Do
they think I have hurt Caroline, possibly even killed her? Is this just about
overstaying my visa? I DON'T KNOW!

Nor can you fully understand until you live the rest of that unlived life
you chose to visit. Is that what you want to do?

I chose to visit? I didn't choose anything.

You chose to commit suicide. You are fortunate to be now allowed to live
the one immortal life you would most like to live. The first choice you made
put you in Caracas with people you chose to be with for the length of time you
chose to be there. You can return to that life if you wish. Understand that if
you do, you will experience the consequences of that decision for eternity.

Those words, '...the consequences of that decision for eternity,'
forced Shelly to consider what she had not before. While not understanding all that was happening, she realized the importance of the
decisions she had made to this point, and would make from now on
was far greater than she had imagined.

Do you want to return to your situation in Caracas?

I do not.

Going there was your choice, but you can decide differently now if you like. However, understand that if you do not return to Caracas, you will never know how that unlived life would have turned out. I ask you one final time: Do you want to return to your situation in Caracas?

I do not.

Think about what you would have done differently. Think very carefully about where that would have led you. All your decisions from this point on will lead you to lives you would have lived had you made different choices. Whatever comes of that, the consequences will be yours, leading you to the one unlived life you will live for eternity.

CHAPTER
TEN

NOW WHAT? SOUTH AFRICA, HARDLY BETTER THAN ZIMBABWE, WON'T HAVE me; what do I do? Where else would I prefer to live?

Shelly had no answers. She wished she had applied to one or more other countries for permission to immigrate instead of just South Africa. A country she didn't want to live in, regardless.

Maybe I need to focus on living here the rest of my life. Others do, including many of my friends from school. Why not me?

She paused to reflect as though doing so would demonstrate to herself that she was serious about choosing the right course of action rather than settling for something potentially much worse.

Is that it? Are there no options other than begging some country to accept me or deciding to stay in Zimbabwe forever?

Shelly could reapply to South Africa, providing some new information she hoped would make a difference. What that might be, she couldn't say.

I give up. I am so frustrated by all this. I am a quality person. I've graduated from university, maybe not with a degree that other countries value, but I do! I will not settle for my life here. I will find somewhere else, and if I don't, maybe I will go on an extended holiday.

This last thought turned Shelly a completely different direction. There was another option.

How can I be sure that the country I choose to immigrate to will be the right one? What if I go to all that trouble and find I don't like it any more than I do Zimbabwe? Instead of looking for 'forever,' I will visit possibilities for short periods. If that works out, I'll know more about what they require from immigrants wishing to stay permanently. Where will I start?

Still with no detailed plan in mind, Shelly felt she would have one soon. Rather than applying to second or third choices, she would visit first-choice countries, those with reasonable tourist visa requirements. At the top of that list was the UK.

I would love to see the UK as a tourist. I believe I would enjoy living there full-time. Maybe one day I will be accepted as a permanent resident. Why not?

Shelly spent the rest of the afternoon reviewing UK requirements for travel with a tourist visa and as an immigrant wishing to settle there permanently. She found visiting was not at all difficult. A simple matter of having sufficient financial resources to pay for her stay and a return ticket to Zimbabwe when her trip was done.

Requesting permanent resident status was another matter. She needed to have a full-time employment offer from a UK company for a position her employer could demonstrate they had been unable to fill with UK citizen applicants. Without that, she would need to build a case for how she would add value to the UK economy in some other way.

I have enough money for a reasonable time away. I deserve a holiday. I can combine being on holiday with exploring employment possibilities that would enable me to move there full-time. It would have to be that. I don't have enough money to invest in an existing business or start one of my own.

Shelly focused on UK tourist destinations most likely to accept her for immigration. The outlook for both looked better than she expected.

London would be at or near the top of the list for any tourist. It certainly is for me. And I now know the percentage of foreign-born residents residing in London is over twice that of the area with the second-highest percentage. I don't know what they'll think of my process operations university degree. It can't be any worse than it has been for South African immigration. I'll worry about that later.

She scouted for locations she would like to see as a tourist. Those she hoped would give her the best opportunity of being accepted as an immigrant. So many options were available for the time and cost she could afford. The final list would be London, Bristol, Manchester, and Edinburgh.

CHAPTER
ELEVEN

PLANNING HER TRIP THE PAST THREE WEEKS DID MUCH TO HELP SHELLY GET past the disappointment of having been rejected by South Africa. She focused on her holiday, finishing packing for what she planned would be three wonderful weeks.

I am ready to go, so happy I decided not to go to Venezuela, particularly this time of year. Too hot and humid. The UK will suit me much better, regardless of whether I can immigrate. I leave the day after tomorrow. It can't come soon enough!

"I can see you are excited, Shelly. Any doubt you will come back?" Miles, her landlord, asked. Shelly knew she had said more than she should have about her trip, causing him to ask this question.

"It shows, does it? Yes, I'll be back. This is just a holiday I've needed more than I knew. Keep an eye on my place, will you, Miles?"

"Of course. Don't concern yourself with anything here; have a good time."

———

Shelly checked her bag for the Kenya Air flight from Harare, Zimbabwe, to London to accomplish three goals. One, get her to London. Two, paying the least amount possible. Three, spending her first night sleeping on the plane rather than in a hotel. While she was confident she had sufficient funds for the trip, some economy along the way would ensure that she did.

Now in her seat, minutes from the 2:40 AM departure time, Shelly sighed, thinking more about what was ahead rather than behind. She quickly fell asleep.

———

How do you feel about this, Shelly? Any regrets about not choosing to go to Venezuela?

It would have been interesting, but no, this feels much more like what I should be doing. Venezuela would have just been a holiday. I would never have considered immigrating there. Actually, not the UK either. I didn't think there was much chance they would accept me. I know there is a lot I need to learn before submitting my immigration request, but I am more confident. This might be where I end up. I hope it is.

———

Shelly slept a few hours, just enough to end the night and begin the morning portion of the flight. Breakfast finished, the trays and dishes picked up, flight attendants passed out the arrival form each passenger must complete prior to their customs interview. On the ground, Shelly quickly went through the arrival formalities and was soon on the Heathrow Express train to Paddington Station, followed by what the booking service said would be a short walk to her hostel, Atlas Studios. Still tired but very happy so far.

I'm in London! I can't believe it. Everything will work out fine. I know it will.

———

"Excuse me, is this seat taken?"

Looking out the window, Shelly heard the voice before looking to see who was speaking. When she did, she saw a young man about her age waiting for an answer. She quickly reached for the jacket she had left on the seat he asked about.

"Sorry, I was daydreaming, looking out the window. No, it's not taken, please sit down."

"Thank you. My name is Lionel, Lionel Katz if you prefer a last name along with the first," he reached out, offering to shake hands, a gesture Shelly thought was funny. Something that would happen between adults much older than they were.

"Nice to meet you, Lionel, I'm Shelly Bennett," she said, accepting and shaking his hand.

"Do you live in London? I'm here on holiday. I live in Israel."

Where he lived somewhat surprised Shelly for reasons she couldn't say. She hoped it wasn't apparent to Lionel.

"I don't live here, but I hope to someday. I'm on holiday as well, looking for places within the UK to immigrate."

Shelly wondered if she had said too much. What if Lionel is some sort of immigration policeman looking to trap those overstaying their tourist visas?

"I just got off the plane a little more than two hours ago. Everything is so new to me," she said, hoping this would somehow eliminate her as a potential visa violator.

"I can guess how tired you are. I certainly was after my flight here three days ago. And that was only six hours. Where do you live?"

"Harare, Zimbabwe."

"I'm embarrassed to say I don't exactly know where that is. I believe in Africa, but where I don't know."

"Most people don't. In the very southern part of the continent, just above Botswana and South Africa, the country."

"How long of a flight was that for you?

"Very long, about sixteen hours total with one stop to refuel. Fortunately, I slept for much of it."

"Isn't, or wasn't, Zimbabwe a member of the British Empire? Not knowing where it is, I confess to not knowing as much as some teachers probably attempted to teach me in school. No point in not admitting it now. If you haven't figured that out, you will shortly."

Shelly liked Lionel's humor and was pleased he decided to sit with her.

"Don't get me started about Zimbabwe's history, particularly what the country is today. You are right to a point, it was a British colony before achieving independence."

"I will do my best not to forget or muck up much of what you've taught me on this short trip. We're pulling into Paddington Station soon, my stop. Where are you headed?

"I'm getting off there as well; my hostel is supposedly close by."

"Mine is too. Maybe I can do a better job directing you to yours than I have demonstrating my knowledge of Africa and Zimbabwe. Where are you staying?"

Shelly paused again before answering, unsure she should give that information to someone she had just met, regardless of how humorous she found him to be.

"Atlas Studios. I believe it's just a few minutes' walk from the station. I shouldn't have any trouble finding it."

Lionel laughed, "No, you certainly won't, and I hope you won't mind me walking with you. I've been a guest there since arriving last Tuesday."

While this might have made Shelly feel better knowing she would not have trouble finding her hostel, she still had a somewhat uneasy feeling about everything related to Lionel since meeting him. But she also accepted that coincidences do happen and decided this was one of them.

"How funny is that? I've taught you something about my country, and you can now repay me by making sure I get where I'm going."

CHAPTER
TWELVE

LIONEL CARRIED ONE OF SHELLY'S TWO BAGS AS THEY WALKED TO THE hostel, engaging in more small talk.

Better we talk about inconsequential things. But he did tell me he was getting off at Paddington before I said I was. I need to be cautious but not overly so.

They reached the hostel, and after checking in, Shelly found her room was two floors above Lionel's. She assumed the floor in between for couples was a buffer separating the single women and men above and below.

Lionel helped Shelly with her luggage to her room, where the two of them found her roommate, Careen. She thanked Lionel, wondering how to end the ongoing discussion between them that began on the train. Not because she hadn't found him interesting. It was awkward with a third person neither of them knew. Or so Shelly assumed.

"So, Lionel, still the unofficial hostel porter, I see."

"I am, Careen, and don't forget, you never tipped me as you said you would."

Somewhat surprised, Shelly joined their conversation, "You two know each other?"

"If helping Careen with her luggage when she arrived, and sitting together at breakfast the next morning, qualifies as knowing each other..." he looked back to Careen, smiling, "...I guess you could say we do. I'll leave the two of you alone to get to know each other. Must go see who else needs my help."

Not sure what to make of the relationship between Careen and Lionel, Shelly thanked him again as he left and closed the door.

Immediately after, the two of them alone, Shelly felt awkward with Careen, wondering if she thought the same about her. How well did she and Lionel know each other? Was it just a coincidence the two of them were assigned the same room? What did Careen think when she came into the room with Lionel? All questions with no answers to this point.

Careen broke the silence.

"Was Lionel just hanging out in the lobby when you came in? He was when I met him."

"No, we were both on the train to Paddington. He asked if he could sit in the empty seat across from me."

"I'm not completely sure about him. He seems very friendly, offering to help. He brought my luggage to my room as he did yours."

"And he helped me with mine to the hostel when we both got off the train at Paddington. Very helpful! Being honest, I was kind of concerned about him, as though he might be a stranger with something on his mind other than just being helpful. But then I remembered, he told me Paddington was his station before I said it was mine. Should we be concerned about him?"

Smiling, Careen replied. "I don't think so. He's just one of those guys who likes helping others. Where are you from, Shelly?"

"Zimbabwe. And you?"

"Morocco. Not close to you, but at least the same continent. How long will you be here?"

"Three full days before leaving for Bristol, then off to Manchester. A few days in each, then north to Edinburgh. How about you, are you on holiday?"

"No, unfortunately, another two days here before going to Cambridge for school. I'm excited to start, but I envy your holiday. Hopefully, I'll do something like that during my time in the UK."

"Cambridge? Wow, very impressive, what will you be studying?'

"Political Science, or at least that's what it will be to start. I'm not sure if I see myself in politics, business, or, in some way, both. Time will tell."

"I'm on holiday, but there is a bit more to it than just that," Shelly said. "I hope to migrate to the UK. I can't qualify to do that now, so I'm using a tourist visa to explore the area, hopefully finding a company that might need me. Not likely, but I'll have fun trying."

"Did you graduate from university?"

"I did, process operations. I believe other countries call it something else, having to do with logistics, management, operations, in general."

"Well, here's wishing both of us good luck! Do you have dinner plans tonight? If not, how about we go together and toast our future success, whatever that will be?"

"Sounds good to me. I'll unpack, shower, and change clothes."

CHAPTER
THIRTEEN

DINNER WITH CAREEN WAS MOSTLY SMALL TALK ABOUT THEIR PASTS, WHAT they hoped for in the future, and a bit more about Lionel. Shelly learned Careen was not interested in him, just someone she met when she arrived at the hostel. Her boyfriend is back in Morocco, but what would come of that, being apart for most of the next four to five years, she couldn't say.

At least I don't have to worry about Careen and Lionel being a couple. Lionel is interesting, but it's too early to think of him as being anything other than someone I will know for the few days we'll both be in London. He'll go home to Israel, I'll continue on my holiday, and after that, who knows where I'll be? And he could have someone waiting for him when he goes home; he might even be married. I don't know, so it's best to focus on why I came here.

Dinner over, Careen and Shelly went back to their shared room. Now, in their beds, they continued their conversation in the dark until Careen noticed that Shelly was no longer responding. Traveling through multiple time zones caught up with her. She was fast asleep.

———

Shelly awoke the next morning feeling very refreshed. Seeing Careen still asleep, she quietly dressed and went downstairs for breakfast.

Exactly what I needed. A good dinner, good conversation, and an uninterrupted night's sleep.

"Since you allowed me to sit next to you on the train, do I need to ask if I can sit at your table?"

The question came from behind Shelly as she sat eating her breakfast. She recognized the voice.

"I don't know, will I have to tip you if I let you join me? Or better still, will you tip me?"

"I'll tip you," Lionel said as he sat down. "What did you do for dinner last night?"

"Careen and I ate together at a place close by. Mimos. Quite good. I guess it's Italian with a UK slant. Owned by a Scillian couple, so of course, we had to drink Peroni's. We certainly laughed a lot. What about you?"

"Nothing as fun as the two of you had. Do you have plans for tonight? If not, why don't the three of us go out? How do the Americans say it? Dutch treat."

"Really? What does that mean?"

"We each pay separately."

"Americans say that? Interesting. Careen has plans tonight, but if you like, I'll have dinner with you, Dutch treat. Where would you like to go?"

"Great! There is a fun place not too far from here, Bondi Green, which serves Australian food, similar to American food. Meat, potatoes, vegetables, or something light such as soup or salad. What do you think?"

"Fine with me. What time, and how dressy do I need to be?"

"Let's meet in the lobby at six, not dressy at all. It's across from Paddington Station, so you know how much of a walk it will be. Not bad. Pick your shoes with that in mind."

"Shoes are not a problem for me. I only have two pairs, and one of them is for job interviews, should I be fortunate enough to get any."

"Job interviews? I thought you were on holiday."

"I am, but I'm also looking at places I might want to live if I receive permission to immigrate. I probably won't have any interviews, but you never know."

"No, you never do. Well, I have a full day ahead of me that starts right now. I look forward to meeting you in the lobby at six. Enjoy your day."

Lionel took his dishes and tray to the kitchen cart by the door, looking back at Shelly as he did. She didn't look up, but she was thinking about him a lot.

CHAPTER
FOURTEEN

SHELLY PLANNED TO DO MORE SIGHTSEEING BUT DECIDED TO READ AND relax in her room instead. She wanted to be rested for dinner with Lionel. While she had a book she was enjoying, tonight's dinner distracted her so much that she put it down, thinking she would sleep. When that did not happen, she gave up and wondered how her time with Lionel would turn out.

What is this about? I've just met him, and I'm thinking...what? That we'll have a relationship? Ridiculous, we're at opposite ends of the earth, living entirely different lives. That's not conducive to anything other than friendship until we go back to life as we planned it. When that happens, it, whatever it is, is over.

She tried thinking about anything other than tonight's dinner, which wasn't possible. The best she could come up with was planning what she would wear, momentarily considering going out looking for something new.

What am I thinking? I have to watch what I spend. I'm not buying any clothes unless it is absolutely necessary. Tonight's dinner does not fall into that category.

Her mind wandered enough so that she fell asleep. The long flight and dinner out last night caught up with her. She awoke a couple of hours later, panicked that she might have overslept.

My God, what time is it? How could I have allowed myself to sleep this long?

A quick look at her watch told her there was still plenty of time to get ready for dinner. Her thoughts returned to what this all meant, but unlike before she fell asleep, her mind now rested, she had a better perspective on things.

I don't get to choose everything. There are times I need to let my life happen. This is one of them. We will have dinner. We'll both enjoy it. What comes of it, I will know at some point after tonight.

While not meeting Lionel for another three hours, Shelly could wait no longer to get dressed. She gathered her things, went to the restroom to shower, and fix her hair. She put on casual clothes she would wear until changing for dinner. Time passed slowly, and finally, at 4:30, she decided to dress to be ready to meet Lionel at six.

———

"Shelly, you look great!" Lionel said as she approached him, sitting in a lobby chair.

"I apologize. I lost track of time. I'm a little late. I hope that doesn't cause a problem for our reservation."

What would he say if he knew I've been ready for close to an hour, pacing the room, hoping to come down and find him waiting for me?

"No problem, no reservation required. Bondi is fashionably casual. How did your day go?"

"As I hoped it would. I caught up on my reading and slept a bit, recovering from jet lag. That's all good and well, but then I started thinking that tomorrow I need to do what I came to London to do. A little sightseeing, but also learning what I can about companies that might consider hiring me, including sponsoring my immigration application."

"I don't know much about the job search part, but I do know about sightseeing. What is your plan? How can you do both?"

"I don't know. I wish I did, but I don't. I haven't been here long, and the little time I have has all been about enjoying myself, including tonight."

Surprised she was so open, she decided to continue.

"You're on holiday, do you mind me asking, from what? What do you do for a living in Israel? Are you in a relationship with anyone?"

She shocked herself, having said this last part.

"Oh, Lionel, I apologize. That is none of my business. I am sorry."

Lionel was surprised, but not about what she said as much as her instant regret having said it.

"Shelly, there's nothing to apologize for. We'll share things about ourselves, that's normal. I have with others I've met here, and now with you. I'll ask questions about you. I hope you won't be offended. If you are, just let me know that's something you'd rather not discuss. I will understand."

More than his words, the way he said them calmed Shelly. She could tell he was more comfortable at this point in his life than she was in hers.

He continued.

"Your questions about what I do, any relationships I might be in, are reasonable, nothing so personal that I wouldn't discuss it with you. I grew up near Be'er-Sheva, a large city in the Negev desert in southern Israel. My family still lives there. I completed undergraduate studies at Tel Aviv University with a degree in liberal arts. As my father said would happen, I quickly learned that would not help me find a job. As a result, I continued my education, completing a Global Sofaer MBA at TAU a little over a year ago. After that, I joined a startup a friend of mine was struggling to make successful. He handles the technical part, I take care of the business end of things. I would tell you more, but our product is related to Israeli security. I cannot speak about it to anyone outside the company."

Shelly realized Lionel had, in little time, become far more real to her.

Yesterday, I questioned whether I could trust him. Today, that concern is gone.

"You also asked if I was in a personal relationship with anyone. I am not. I was too busy with school to have been, or the right person never appeared, maybe both. Now that I'm done with school, I have little time for anything other than helping my partner, Amir, start our business. Did I miss anything? I will answer any questions you have about me, excluding work-related matters. But right now, we should start towards dinner to be on time. Ok?"

"Certainly, thank you for being so open with me, Lionel. I am embarrassed that I have not been with you. I will be at dinner."

———

Bondi was much better than Shelly expected, both the food and the restaurant itself. So open and bright, the people all so beautiful, dressed so nicely. She began intimidated by it all, but soon concentrated on her conversation with Lionel, telling him about herself as he had done at the hostel.

What does this all mean? In less than a day and a half, have I met someone I see as more than just a friend? Am I willing to change my plans to find out? I have less than two days to decide before leaving London.

Dinner over, Lionel suggested they move to a cafe close to Atlas for a drink before heading back to the hostel. Shelly agreed, and once there, the conversation continued.

"What an incredible night this has been, don't you think, Shelly? By incredible, I mean I did not expect either of us would discuss such intimate details of our lives. Why would we? We're both leaving soon, with different futures ahead of us. I don't know about you, so I will answer for myself. I feel something for you, my brain tells me I shouldn't. More than I feel for others I've met on this trip, as well as those back in Israel. I'm guessing you may feel something similar for me. If you do, we at least owe it to each other to be honest about our feelings. If we had more time together, we could just let things happen. That isn't the case. Please tell me what you are thinking, including you not seeing things as I do, if that is how you feel."

Shelly looked away from Lionel when he finished. She could say she had thoughts similar to his, but decided not to, at least not tonight.

"We do have much to consider, Lionel. This is happening very quickly for both of us. Let's head back to the hostel. I want to think about tonight and what you've said before I respond. Are you okay with that?"

"Certainly, and I will do the same."

CHAPTER
FIFTEEN

WHAT DO YOU THINK?

He was honest with me, I feel something for him, but am I ready to give up my plan? He told me how he feels, but not what he thinks we should do. I want to hear what that is.

Suppose what he thinks would require you to stop looking for a job, and your hope to immigrate to the UK. What then?

That's the problem, I don't know.

You don't know what? Would your feelings for him be so strong that you would change your plans? Or you don't know what you need to know to decide?

I don't know.

Shelly, when there is conflict between your brain and your heart, you must sometimes choose to do that which is most painful for you. This is one of those times. Sleep now, your dreams will lead you to the correct conclusion. You will know if it is time to leave this place, person, or situation.

CHAPTER
SIXTEEN

SHELLY AWOKE, REFRESHED, BELIEVING SHE HAD DREAMED SOMETHING critical to her future. However, precisely what that was, she could not recall.

It almost certainly has something to do with Lionel, but what was it?

She hoped to meet him at breakfast and got up to get ready. In less than an hour, she went downstairs and into the dining area, where she saw him sitting by himself. He looked up, smiling as she walked toward him.

"How did you sleep?" Lionel asked, watching Shelly approach.

"Better than I thought I would, how about you?"

"Being honest, not good; too much on my mind."

"Yes, well, also being honest, the same for me. But I did eventually fall asleep and woke up feeling good this morning, until I thought about last night. Lionel, I appreciate you being so honest and open with me about us. I have thoughts about that as well. I hoped I would get to a place where it would be easy for me to respond to you this morning. That did not happen, and I keep coming back to what I believe is the center of our problem. My heart is telling me one thing, my brain another. I don't know which I should listen to more. I have a question. Am I right assuming we both must decide whether or not it is time to leave this place, each other, and our situation?"

Lionel did not hesitate to answer.

"Yes, and there is a great risk to our futures depending on what we decide. We must do that independently of each other. What each of us wants will not happen unless we want the same thing. Based on that, can you tell me what you thought about what I said last night? Keep in mind, Shelly, we have so little time together; if you can't answer sometime today, that is a response."

"I can't believe what I'm about to say. We don't know nearly enough about each other or us as a couple to alter our plans. Our lives are headed in very different directions. However," Shelly took a deep breath before continuing. "I can change my plans if I decide to do so. Whether or not I should is another matter. I may never be able to immigrate to the UK, or anywhere else I'd like to live." She paused again, looking briefly to her left before turning back to Lionel.

"As of this moment, and please don't let this scare you, I believe you may be the one person I should be with, potentially forever. But I don't know that for certain, and I need to be certain before making an irreversible commitment to myself and to you. There is only one way to find out how much we want to be together, and that is to be together. If you agree, Lionel, and what you ask of me is something I can agree to do, I will change my plans to match yours."

Shelly's response stunned Lionel. He wanted to hear that he meant something to her, but did not expect what she just said.

"I'm shocked, Shelly! Surprised more than I thought possible, but very happy as well. I care a great deal about you as well, but you are right, we both have questions and doubts. I should have said something similar last night. I will now. I want us to be together. Can we find some way to make that happen? Something that suits us both. I have to go back to my job in Israel. It sounds as though you can alter your plans. Will you come to Israel with me? If not when I return, soon after. You can stay with me, or separately, whichever you prefer. Being together will teach each of us a great deal about our relationship. This is very important to us both. Please take enough time to be certain how you answer."

Shelly sat thinking about what she said and Lionel's reaction.

"I need to be alone while I think this through. I hope you understand. I will take a walk; can we meet in the lobby around eleven? That will give me the time I need to answer you. And if I am still not certain, as you said, that will be a response."

"Absolutely, Shelly," Lionel said as he stood to leave. "Take whatever time you need. I will be here when you return."

CHAPTER
SEVENTEEN

SHELLY LEFT THE HOSTEL, WALKING TOWARD HYDE PARK, CONTINUING ON a path paralleling Carriage Drive through the park toward Serpentine Lake. Home to Kensington Gardens, adjacent to Kensington Palace and Buckingham Palace, Shelly found it to be the perfect place to sort out her thoughts as she walked alone.

The right location to question the place, person, and situation.

She came to a bench overlooking the lake and sat down.

What will I do? Whatever it will be, there is more I don't know than that I do. Nothing is assured. Any decision I make about staying with my plan or moving to Israel may not work out for Lionel and me. So what will it be, Shelly?

What my father used to tell me certainly applies now.

'You won't always know all you need to know to decide what you should do or not do. Consider everything carefully, including having some idea of what you will do if things do not turn out as you hope. When you have done that, make your decision and move ahead.'

That makes deciding what to do very easy. I don't know anything close to all I need to know. But what will I do if things aren't as I hoped? I could leave Israel, move back to Zimbabwe, and make new plans there. Or, if I like Israel, maybe I will choose to remain there without Lionel.

She paused to consider her options.

Sure, why not; either or both could work at least for me. I will tell Lionel that with the rest of my decision. I cannot go with him when he returns. I need time to go home to close out my apartment, get rid of what I will not take to Israel, and say goodbye to friends and family. I will have to work in Israel. Lionel will know something about that and may be able to help me find something once I'm there. If that works for him, and with everything else done, I will join him in Israel. I will not stay with him. We need more time to get to know each other. I need to find a job. I have limited resources to support myself. I will ask if he can help me with some of that, should it be necessary. This is my plan, but it must also become his plan for it to work.

Shelly felt the weight of indecision and doubt had been lifted from her. While she had more time to think sitting in the park, she now wanted to share her thoughts with Lionel as soon as possible.

———

Back in the hostel, Shelly went to Lionel's room and knocked on the door. She heard footsteps coming to answer and was relieved it was him, not his roommate.

"Shelly, you're back sooner than I expected. Did you take enough time to think things through?"

"Yes, I did. I have a plan, and if you're ready to listen, I will tell you what it is."

"I am, and I want to know what you think. We can go somewhere to talk, or you're welcome to come in. My roommate is gone for the day."

"I was in Hyde Park, it's so pretty and peaceful there; it helped me see things, deciding what to do. Let's go there."

"Great, let me get my shoes on. I'll meet you in the lobby in ten minutes."

———

Lionel came down the stairs to the lobby less than five minutes later. They left for the park, Shelly leading the way.

"I'll get to the details once we find a place to sit and talk, but let me tell you more about how I got to where I am. I thought about my father and how he told me to approach making critical life-changing decisions. It comes down to this. Consider everything very carefully, and nothing more than what to do if things *don't* work out as you hope. Have a backup plan. Once you've done that, decide what you'll do and go ahead. I've done that, Lionel. You might think I didn't take enough time to be sure. You'd be right; I didn't because neither of us knows enough to say with certainty that I should move to Israel to be with you. So, as my father taught me, all we can do is focus on what I will do if things between us do not work out."

Lionel looked ahead, not responding as they continued walking. Shelly wanted to sit on the same bench she had earlier, if possible. When they reached it, she was happy to see it empty.

"When I sat on this bench a little over two hours ago, I didn't know what I would do. Shortly after, once again, recalling what my father told me, I suddenly did. Lionel, I care for you enough to decide I will move to Israel. I will give our relationship the time it needs for both of us to know whether it will work. But there are some details you need to know and accept. I must first return to Zimbabwe to close out my life there. That will take a month, maybe more. I will need to find a job in Israel. I hope you can help me do that. I have sufficient funds to take care of myself without a job for three months after I arrive. If nothing happens by then, but I am optimistic that it will with more time, I will need some support in the form of a loan. I don't know anyone else to look to for that other than you. And while I do not want to think so, that might be money I must use to return to Zimbabwe should we mutually agree that things are not working out between us. Should that happen, any money you provide for any reason is a loan I will repay in the future. Finally, it is best that we live separately until we get to know each other better. What do you think?"

Lionel looked at kids playing with boats at the lake shore, waiting a short while before turning back toward Shelly, smiling as he did.

"I couldn't have come up with a better plan, and I like the possibility of you needing some financial help. While everything you've said may turn out as we both hope beyond a trial period, there will be times when things are not going well for one or both of us. Better to experience that as part of the trial rather than after. I agree with all you've said."

CHAPTER
EIGHTEEN

LIFE'S FUNNY, ISN'T IT? WE PLAN, THINGS CHANGE, WE MAKE NEW PLANS, and in the end, we don't know if what is, is better than what might have been.
Why does that sound so familiar?
You don't recall now, Shelly, but you will one day.

———

Having decided to move to Israel, Shelly concentrated on all she needed to do before joining Lionel in Tel Aviv. In some respects, the task was easy because she had little to give up. She sold or gave away everything she would not take with her, keeping only her clothes and some personal family remembrances. What was proving difficult was telling some of her friends what she was doing and why she was doing it. And none more so than her close friend, Eve.

———

"You're joking!"

"No, Eve, I'm not, I'm going to Israel."

"Shelly, you went to the UK for a holiday and to see if you might be successful applying to immigrate there, that I understand. You were there less than a week, all that time in one city. You meet a guy from

Israel, you like each other, and all of a sudden, you're moving to Israel to be with him? You don't think that sounds like a joke, maybe even crazy?"

Eve's theatrics made Shelly laugh, but she understood why she reacted as she did. Every person she told what she was doing had a similar reaction. And late at night, the closer she got to leaving, Shelly second-guessed her plan as well.

"I understand, Eve, I do. There is no way I can make this sound rational. It isn't to me, it isn't to Lionel, but it is what we both want. We can't try to have a relationship living so far apart. It won't work. We must be close to each other. We plan to be together to see if something more than infatuation results. If it doesn't, I will move back to Zimbabwe or elsewhere."

"Well, it is your life, Shelly, but I'm very concerned for you. Please let me know how things are progressing. If you need any help, do not hesitate to ask. I will do whatever I can."

"Thank you, Eve. You are such a good friend, I knew I could count on you. I will write you often and look forward to hearing from you."

———

The day Shelly was to leave finally arrived. Eve drove her to Harare International Airport, still questioning whether she wanted to reconsider her decision. Once there, she helped Shelly check her luggage into the terminal. With that done, they both knew for sure, Shelly was leaving.

"Shelly, how can you be so calm about all of this? I'm a mess thinking about what may happen."

"I know, Eve, and being honest, I'm nervous too. But I have a backup plan, I hope I don't need. If I do, I will use it, and you will be one of the first to hear about it. Give me a hug once more, sweetheart, and thanks for all you've done for me, and your friendship. We will see each other again."

The goodbyes over, Shelly walked toward security, looking over her shoulder one last time to see Eve wiping tears from her eyes. She had to look away.

———

Less than six weeks ago, I was on long flights with layovers to London. Now here I am again doing much the same to a completely different place, person, and situation. Maybe Eve is right. Perhaps I am crazy.

But Shelly reminded herself that one thing would be very different. Lionel was meeting her at Tel Aviv airport. That thought calmed her considerably, so much so that she slept for much of the first leg of the journey. After a three-hour layover in Ethiopia, she was on the plane again, too excited to sleep. Soon, she and Lionel would begin finding out how crazy they are.

Once landed, Shelly made her way through the Israeli arrival process, which she found to be much more stringent than any she had experienced in other airports.

I suppose it must be given Israel's history with its Arab neighbors. One more thing I will have to adjust to.

She claimed her luggage, put it on a cart, and moved to customs, expecting more detailed questions and searches of her two suitcases. But Israeli customs proved to be no more extensive than she had experienced elsewhere. She was free to exit to where those meeting arriving passengers would be waiting.

Walking through the door leading from customs, she heard Lionel calling her name before she could find him among the many people looking for their friends and family.

"Shelly, over here, Shelly!"

She looked to the left and saw him smiling, waving in her direction. All she needed to do now was pass through one last barrier separating arrivals from those waiting for them, and they would be together.

I still can't believe it. Less than six weeks ago, I was questioning what I should do. And now, here I am, in Israel, beginning an entirely new chapter in my life.

CHAPTER
NINETEEN

SHELLY SETTLED IN THE HOTEL WHERE SHE WOULD STAY WHILE LOOKING FOR something more permanent. She thought she would begin looking for a job immediately; however, Lionel had other ideas. He would introduce her to Israel, in general, and Tel Aviv, in particular, showing her many of the sites visited by tourists from all over the world. He was proud of both and wanted her to enjoy his country and adopted city as much as he did.

Lionel's apartment was within walking distance of the company he and his partner were creating. He knew that to be both a blessing and a curse. Not having to commute to work, as his partner did, he often worked late because he lived nearby, and believed that is what one does in a startup.

Soon after arriving in Tel Aviv, Shelly rented an apartment near Lionel's building, settled in, and was enjoying her time with only one concern. After the first two weeks of being there, Lionel explained he would have to spend more time at work rather than continuing to show her the city and surrounding area.

I knew this would happen; he has to go back to work. It was great while it lasted, but it's time we put sightseeing aside and begin living like most people do. Part of our evolving relationship. And I need to concentrate on finding a job. I've had two good offers, and expect there will be more. It's about more than the money; I want to look forward to going to work. Lionel doesn't appear to be concerned that I haven't found what I'd like to do. He's being very patient.

But the topic did come up over a late dinner on a Sunday night after Lionel had once again worked all weekend.

"I feel guilty knowing I haven't helped you look for a job. It's not that I don't want to, I do. I've been so busy, and there doesn't appear to be a let-up anytime soon. So much to do, so little time to get it all done."

"I completely understand. There is no need to apologize. I am very optimistic about my job search. I've had two good offers. I won't accept either one just yet. I want to make sure I find the right one for me. You concentrate on your company, and I will take care of myself. I would like more time with you, but we both need to focus on our careers, possibly a little more than our relationship. I'm okay with that. Since we're on the subject, how are things going for you? I don't mean the technology; I know you can't discuss that. Just the 'getting things going' part."

"Thank you, Shelly. It helps a lot having you near, being as understanding as you are. As for how the company is doing, we have made much progress with the technology, that isn't the challenge. Establishing the processes we need to function as a growing company is the issue. HR, production, sales, finance, accounting, etc. I know a little to a lot about most of that, but I only have so much time to devote to any of it. I need help. Amir is a tech guy, by his own admission, not well-suited to running a business. And then there is the question of how much an operations person would cost. Financially, we are fine, but there is a limit to how much we can afford to pay for help. I'm not sure what we will do."

Shelly thought about what Lionel said. Her degree was in process operations, exactly the area Lionel says they need the most help. She had no senior-level manager experience, but had worked with others who did, learning quite a lot.

"Lionel, I will suggest something you can immediately dismiss if you like. Maybe you should; I'm not convinced what I'm thinking would work. And even if you are okay with it, Amir may not be. My degree is in process operations, the term used in Zimbabwe that encompasses all and more you say you are struggling to organize. I don't have senior-level management experience, but I have been a mid-level manager following a plan I helped create. What if I came to work for you, helping you organize and implement an operations plan? I won't cost as much as a senior-level employee, and we each would gain personal experience working together. That will not be true if you hire a stranger, and I work elsewhere. It might benefit us both and the company."

There was more she wanted to say, but felt it was best to let Lionel consider the suggestion. To see if he thought the two of them working together was a good idea. He looked at Shelly as she spoke, and when she stopped, he did not immediately respond. Shelly became concerned, thinking she hadn't given him a way out.

"You can simply say no, I won't be offended. We will still have our time together. That's going so well, I don't want to do anything to upset it."

"I understand, Shelly. That isn't why I haven't answered. I am thinking about what you said, how it might work, and how it would impact us personally. A great idea if we did not have a personal relationship. It might still be, I hope it is. You are right, Amir would have to agree to try it. We would have to agree on your compensation, and you and I would have to seriously think about you working with me—I do not want to call it working for me—what it would do to us away from work. Those are all just questions now, but it might work. Let's both think and talk about it more in the next day or so. If you are okay with it, I would like to discuss it with Amir tomorrow. He often says you are special, telling me not to do anything to lose you. Maybe your suggestion will put that to the test."

———

A week or so after many lengthy discussions of how Shelly joining the company might work, she became the company's first non-partner employee. Doing so immediately helped more than Shelly or Lionel expected. What she did accelerated growth, including hiring three more employees, two of whom reported to her.

Soon after, the company relocated to the outskirts of Netanya for a lower cost of living, including lower facility costs. They were now closer to other tech startups while still in proximity to Tel Aviv when required to be there. As a bonus, the quality of life associated with living in a vibrant community located on the shores of the Mediterranean Sea was significantly better than it had been in Tel Aviv. Shelly and Lionel went from working for an uncertain startup to being key managers of an early-stage company, attempting to manage problems resulting from too much growth too quickly.

Lionel now had more time away from work, which benefited both him and Shelly. Their personal relationship no longer in doubt; they married a little more than a year after she joined him in Tel Aviv. And while not requested to do so by Lionel or his family, Shelly had another surprise for him. She applied for Israeli citizenship and was in the process of converting to Judaism. Life was good with one major concern.

CHAPTER
TWENTY

"THE COMPANY IS PROGRESSING ACCORDING TO OUR PLAN, LIONEL. THE one you and I, along with Amir, created. Employees added, growth continues, and after two years of marriage, we are finally financially in a position to consider having a baby. This is no snap decision. We have discussed it throughout our relationship, making certain each of us is aware of the other's feelings. I'm getting older, you are too. The time to have a baby is now or never."

Shelly paused to allow Lionel to respond, and when he didn't, she continued.

"We have it all worked out, with one exception. Do you have any second thoughts about your decision to join the Israel Defense Forces?"

"I don't, Shelly, for the reasons I've shared with you so often."

"I know, but doesn't us now planning to have a child, finally being in a position to have one, change things? Your country thinks so; they exempt married men from compulsory service. You don't have to go, Lionel, and you are more valuable to Israel growing your company."

"That's also true for hundreds of thousands of others who serve even when they are no longer required to do so. I couldn't live with myself if I didn't, and I don't believe you could, either. Remember, it's now *your* country, too. No, Shelly, I haven't changed my mind; it's a matter of self-respect. I must serve as all in my family have in the past."

Lionel began his enlistment, assigned to an IDF military police unit. While the threat of war was always present, Middle East politics, at least that directly affecting Israel, had been relatively quiet since he joined.

He was comfortable with his military life, but he worried, knowing his absence from the company was a problem he could do little about. He thought back to the numerous discussions he had with Shelly about him voluntarily joining the IDF. For Lionel, avoiding it was unacceptable. He was in now and would make the best of it.

About halfway through his enlistment, the First Intifada began at the Jabalia refugee camp. Initially, mostly peaceful demonstrations, work stoppages, and other forms of civil disobedience by Palestinians protesting Israeli occupation forces. Israel reacted by sending an overwhelming number of troops to restore order, including Lionel. While casualties among Israeli military units were minimal relative to those of the Palestinians, Lionel was among them, killed by a single bullet fired by an unseen individual while patrolling a street in the refugee camp.

Shelly did not want Lionel to serve, but she also had not expected him to be killed. Her concern was being without him for the two-plus years he would be gone. And now that time would be forever.

God, WHY? Why him while I continue living? I can't do that, you have no right to take him from me.

You know better than to tell God what right He has to do anything! You committed suicide; who gave you the right to do that? Why did you do that, Shelly? Because you could? How selfish are you? What did I mean when I said you would know when it is time to leave a place, person, or situation?

What did you mean? I don't know. I suppose something I am supposed to know to avoid trouble.

Possibly, but such thinking focuses on the leaving part. Is there something more to it, something that has to do with staying?

I don't know. Why are you hounding me? If you are me, you know? I don't, so you tell me.

You know, Shelly. Think about it. You will understand because you cannot choose not to understand. You will know when it is time to leave a place, person, or situation.

CHAPTER
TWENTY-ONE

Lionel was dead, forever lost to the world and Shelly.

Now, staying with his parents on the fifth day of Lionel's Shiva, Shelly contemplated what to do next.

I can return to Zimbabwe or migrate to another country that accepts Jewish immigrants, particularly those who are financially successful. Lionel left me his share of the business. The company is still young but growing profitably.

Amir wanted her to stay, certainly for the time he would need to find replacements for Lionel and Shelly should she decide to leave.

Lionel's parents made it clear they considered Shelly to be part of their immediate family with a direct connection to Lionel. They wanted her to stay with them as long as she wished.

She knew what they all wanted, but what did *she* want?

I've told Amir I need to grieve. He understood and said I should take whatever time necessary; the company and my position would be waiting for me if I choose to return. I've briefly visited Zimbabwe to see friends, especially Eve. That was good for me, but I cannot live there permanently.

Shelly spent the better part of a year traveling throughout Israel to gain more understanding of her role in Jewish life. She was Jewish, a naturalized citizen of Israel. She found significant meaning and purpose in being that. However, for the moment, and she feared, possibly forever, she felt only loss and grief.

CHAPTER
TWENTY-TWO

"YOU WILL KNOW WHEN IT IS TIME TO LEAVE A PLACE, PERSON, OR *situation.*"

Why does that repeatedly run through my mind? Leave what? Lionel left me. He didn't want to, I know that. But he has left while I am still here. My situation has changed. I am no longer married to Lionel. I did not leave the marriage; he did.

What about your situation, Shelly? Has that left you as well? Or did Lionel's passing take you from your situation?

Yes, it did. He did all of that, and I am angry because he did.

What will you do now? You must decide. Before you do, think about what you can leave. Not Lionel, he no longer exists. Your marriage? No, again, that has ended. Your situation? What is that? If you define it as marriage to Lionel, a very narrow definition. That is over. The only thing you have left to leave is your grief. Put it behind you and move to your immortal future.

I want to, but how do I do that?

You have an infinite number of unlived lives you would have lived had you made different choices. Your time in Venezuela and now with Lionel in Israel are only two of them. You are blessed with the opportunity to visit more if you wish, looking for the one you would choose to be your immortal life.

If I do, who will I be with throughout eternity?

You won't know unless and until you visit more unlived lives. Your choices in mortal life have led you to this crossroads of immortality. You have the opportunity to experience some of your unlived lives to help you choose your immortal life. If you choose not to, you are accepting an immortal fate imposed on you rather than chosen by you. And remember, Shelly, failing to decide is itself a choice.

How do I decide what to do?

You already have.

CHAPTER
TWENTY-THREE

I HAVE TO THINK CAREFULLY ABOUT CUTTING THIS TRIP SHORT, GOING HOME to close out my life in Zimbabwe, before heading off to Israel to join Lionel. A big part of me wants to do that, but what if...

Shelly had lingering doubts about moving to Israel almost from the very first moment she and Lionel came up with their plan.

I was so caught up in everything. I didn't have a plan, and then suddenly, I did. So proud of myself, it never occurred to me that I should think about this more than the couple of hours it took Lionel and me to decide this was what we wanted to do. I trust him, but I don't know why I should after knowing him for such a short time. And what about him? He doesn't know nearly enough about me to decide we should be together, potentially for life. I know our plan is a trial, but what are the odds of it working? I have to talk to him about this more!

Shelly went to Lionel's room and knocked on the door. No one answered, and she wondered what to do next. She had to speak with him today. Things were moving too quickly. She knew he might be making plans he wouldn't otherwise choose to do if he knew what she was thinking. She knocked once more, and with no response, she decided the best and only thing she could do was wait for him in the lobby. Once downstairs, she stopped at the reception desk.

"Excuse me. Have you seen Lionel this morning?"

"Only briefly, he was heading out as I was coming to work."

"Did he say where he was going or when he would be back?'

"No, we just said good morning as we passed. Is there a problem? Maybe I can help you?"

"No, that's alright; I need to talk to him. I'll just wait for him here in the lobby. He'll probably be back shortly."

Morning turned to afternoon. Shelly remained in the lobby, not wanting to chance missing Lionel coming in. She was hungry and thought about getting a quick snack in the dining room, finally deciding against it. They had to talk as soon as he returned, and she didn't want to miss him.

The hours rolled by, and Shelly decided she would leave a note in an envelope she would slip under his door. The desk clerk gave her stationery and a pen, as she requested.

Staring at the blank page, she questioned the very first words she should write.

Do I say, 'Dear Lionel' or just 'Lionel'? If I can't even decide how to address him, how will I ever know all else I should say?

Lionel, we need to talk as soon as possible, tonight, no matter how late. I'm having second thoughts about our plan. I have to discuss it with you. I knocked on your door twice this morning and again now. No answer, so I'm leaving you this note. Please come get me in my room, I'm waiting for you.

Shelly

She read her words, the impersonal beginning and end, in particular.

If I got this note, I would know exactly what the person writing it had in mind.

———

Shelly wasn't sure what time she fell asleep or if Lionel had knocked at her door so quietly she didn't hear him. Now morning, she had slept in her clothes all night, and the talk she so desperately wanted to have with him never occurred.

Not knowing what else to do, she went down the hall to the bathroom, showered, dressed, and was ready for whatever came next. She then went down to the lobby to speak to the desk clerk.

"Are there any messages for me?"

"Let me check. Yes, here's one," he said, handing her an envelope. Having never seen Lionel's handwriting, she wasn't sure it was from him, while knowing it couldn't be from anyone else. She sat down in a nearby chair, opened the envelope, and began to read the message.

Dear Shelly,

I am sorry I missed you yesterday. As you have, I also had much to think about. Too much to do at the hostel, I rented a room nearby for the night, and found your note when I returned early this morning.

I don't know the details of what you wanted to talk about, but I can guess. You are not comfortable changing your plans to join me in Israel. I don't blame you; I am questioning how fast all this is happening as well. We need to slow down.

I've checked out of the hostel and am going back to Israel this afternoon. This is my address in Tel Aviv. I hope you will write me so we can continue discussing our future.

Lionel Katz

Markolet 9.6, Markolet Street

Florentin, Tel Aviv, Israel

Shelly, I care about you greatly. I hope we will pick this up again soon when we've both had time to think about what we want from life and each other.

Lionel

Shelly sat looking at his note, all at once feeling relieved and sad. She had not been looking forward to what she knew would be an uncomfortable conversation. One that now would not take place. But she was also sad thinking he might have talked her into staying with their plan, convincing her all would go as they hoped.

She put the note back in the envelope, got up from the chair, and walked outside. A beautiful day in London, too much so to stay indoors; she began to walk with no destination in mind.

What do I do now? I still have my UK itinerary and am only missing some of the sightseeing I planned to do in London. I don't feel much up to that now after all the chaos of the last two days, but doing some of it may be exactly what I should do. It might help get Lionel and our plans off my mind until I'm ready to focus on just that. And it would undoubtedly be better than canceling everything, returning to Zimbabwe. There's nothing there for me. I don't know. I can't seem to be sure of much of anything. I don't choose what will happen to me as much as I accept what others choose for me.

But not this time. I've booked and paid for this trip. I will go ahead with it. At the very least, I will enjoy time away from Zimbabwe.

CHAPTER
TWENTY-FOUR

SHELLY ENJOYED HER FINAL DAY IN LONDON MORE THAN SHE EXPECTED. Lionel was still on her mind, but she could not ignore all that London had to offer. Having squeezed in as much as she could in her only full day devoted to sightseeing, she had a quick dinner alone and spent the evening preparing for travel to Bristol, her next UK stop.

This trip was supposed to be about more than just sightseeing. Shelly hoped to make a connection that would help her immigrate to the UK. Her landlord in Zimbabwe recommended her to Joyce Chitepo, his accountant, who had a connection in the UK that might be of help to her. The managing director of Africa Universe Adventures (AUA), a travel company headquartered in Bristol. Joyce said she would contact them to see if someone at AUA would agree to meet with Shelly, accepting her CV via fax. No promises, and Shelly would not know until she arrived in Bristol and called to see if a meeting was possible.

Her time in London all but over, she reflected on everything to this point.

I am embarrassed that I decided to move to Israel with little or no thought. But I am also pleased I decided not to before actually going through with it. I have feelings for Lionel, and we may yet decide we want to be together. But if we had gone ahead with our plan, that might have put an end to us as a couple. Tomorrow's train trip to Bristol will give me time to focus on my plan to immigrate to the UK. I will relax, putting aside all that has happened so far, thinking only about what may lie ahead. Once I arrive and get to my hostel, I will call AUA to see if a meeting could be arranged.

———

Shelly awoke the next morning forty minutes before her alarm. She slept soundly, was refreshed, and decided to get up, shower, and dress. She packed the night before and only needed to have breakfast before the short walk back to Paddington Station and her train to Bristol. It was time to leave the last few days behind her, moving towards whatever lay ahead.

The station was full of the usual morning rush of commuters. Not knowing exactly where to be, she was pleased she arrived with plenty of time before her train was scheduled to depart. After a few inquiries, she found the track her train would be leaving on in an hour. Time for a cup of hot tea, followed by a visit to the "loo," as Shelly learned in London, was British for what Americans referred to as a "restroom." Her thoughts immediately returned to Zimbabwe.

Strange how many different terms there are in languages for something so familiar to all of us. Back home, those speaking Shona would refer to it as chimbudzi. My coworker, Adam, who lived in the US for a year as a student, said Americans have many words for it, including slang. Bathroom, head, toilet, outhouse, potty, John. That's a strange one; I wonder how men named John feel about that.

Less than 15 minutes until departure, Shelly heard the announcement to board her train. She gathered her things, climbed aboard, and found a seat. She felt very good about her morning so far and looked forward to her time in Bristol.

The train departed on time, and Shelly enjoyed watching the outskirts of London roll by. Soon, in the countryside, she looked out the window as the train climbed through South Devon Hills and down to the coast with seaside views. She thought she might sleep on the way, but was too interested watching to see what would come next. She didn't want to miss any of it.

———

"Ten minutes to Bristol Temple Meads, ten minutes. Please look around you, gather all your belongings, ready to disembark. The train will depart after a brief stop. Please stay on the train if this is not your station. Ten minutes to Bristol Temple Meads."

Shelly was ready to get off when the train came to a stop. The station was much smaller than Paddington, which meant it was also less confusing. She hoped her hostel would be within walking distance, but that turned out not to be the case. Now in a taxi with non-rush hour traffic, she arrived at her hostel 20 minutes later.

Having completed the check-in process, she asked the desk clerk for help contacting African Universe Adventures.

"Can you help me with this phone call? I believe it's local," Shelly said, handing the clerk the paper with the number to call AUA when she arrived.

"Certainly, and it is a local call. Would you prefer to place the call from your room? If not, you can use this phone if you like," he said, gesturing to a phone at the end of the front desk.

"Thank you. I'm not familiar with placing calls in the UK. Would you mind dialing it for me? I will do it here and will pay for it."

"No need for that, miss. I'm happy to help," he said as he dialed the number on the paper Shelly handed him.

"It's ringing," he said, holding out the receiver for Shelly to take.

"AUA, may I help you?"

"I hope so, my name is Shelly Bennett. I just arrived in Bristol and was told to call to see if your managing director would have time to meet with me regarding a position with your company. I apologize, I do not have his name. This was to be arranged by Miss Joyce Chitepo in my country, Zimbabwe."

"Our managing director is a woman, Evelyn Walker. Please hold, I will check with her."

Shelly regretted not having the connection's name or even knowing whether it was a man or a woman. A few minutes later, the person answering the phone came back on the line.

"Evelyn has been expecting your call. She can see you tomorrow at

9 AM at our office if that works for you. Do you have the address? Are you familiar with Bristol?"

"I don't have the address, and this is my first time in Bristol. But I'm sure a taxi will be able to find it. I have pen and paper and will take down the address."

"We are at 52 Welsh Back. Your driver will have no problem finding it. Is there anything else I can help you with?"

"No, thank you, you've been very helpful. I will be there tomorrow morning, a little before 9 AM."

The call complete, her appointment set, Shelly was ecstatic! Everything to this point worked out perfectly. The trip to Bristol, reaching AUA's office on the phone, and getting an appointment to see the managing director the next morning. Everything much better than she anticipated.

Shelly walked back to the desk clerk, who was standing a few feet away.

"Thank you again, I appreciate your help."

"My pleasure, miss. If there is anything more I can do to help, just let me know."

"Do you know how much time it will take for a taxi to get to 52 Welsh Back tomorrow morning?"

"Depending on what time you need to be there, fifteen to as much as thirty minutes."

"I need to arrive by 8:45 AM."

"Twenty minutes, tops, and taxis will be right out front."

"Perfect! What time is breakfast served?"

"Full breakfast in the dining room, 6:00 to 8:30 AM, or, if you prefer, coffee and rolls here in the lobby until 9:00 AM."

"Also perfect, thank you again."

"You're welcome. Do you need help with your luggage?"

"No, I can handle it. Which way is the elevator?"

"Down that hall behind you, on the left, enjoy your stay."

CHAPTER
TWENTY-FIVE

SHELLY DID NOT SLEEP WELL, THE RESULT OF THINKING TOO MUCH ABOUT her meeting with Ms. Walker this morning. Her alarm was set for 6:30 AM. She gave up trying to sleep and got up at 5:45 to shower and dress. She wondered if there was anything she should do to prepare for the meeting other than bringing copies of her CV. She was confident she could handle all questions about her employment and education history. The one she was most concerned about was why she wanted to immigrate to the UK.

I would ask that if I were Ms. Walker, she probably will as well. What do I say? Nothing so soppy as I've always loved the UK and wanted to become a citizen. Just the truth. The opportunity for advancement in Zimbabwe is limited, particularly for women. I can be an asset to a company and benefit myself if I live somewhere else—something like that. I must not overthink it.

Now 8:00 AM, having had her breakfast, Shelly decided to leave early to ensure she arrived on time. She stopped at the desk to confirm the taxi arrangements.

"I need to get to 52 Welsh Back no later than 8:45 this morning. What's the best way to get a taxi, and about how long do you expect it will take to get there?"

The desk clerk, a different one from the night before, answered.

"They will likely be taxis in the neighborhood. Just stand out front and wave one to stop. Maybe a 15-minute ride."

"Thanks, I'll wait outside enjoying the morning."

Casting aside concern about appearing overanxious, Shelly waved to the first taxi she saw and arrived at AUA shortly after. No company signs on any of the nearby buildings, but she did see the address. She went inside the building lobby and found a tenant listing, including one for African Universe Adventures on the third floor. Right place, a half hour too early, she would spend some time walking close by in the surrounding neighborhood.

Shelly started toward the lobby door just as a woman was coming in. They looked at each other, the other woman more intently at Shelly.

"Excuse me, are you, by chance, Shelly Bennett?"

Startled to hear her name, Shelly replied, "Why, yes, I am."

"Brilliant, I thought you might be. I'm Evelyn Walker; we have an appointment at 9. If you weren't about to do something else, would you like to come up with me now, maybe have a cup of tea or coffee if you like?

Sensing her nervousness, being too early for her appointment, Shelly replied, "No, I mean, yes, I would if that's not a problem for you. I don't have anything else to do until you're ready to see me."

I sound like a foolish teenage girl!

"You being a little early is good for me. We'll have more time to talk, and I can move on to other things sooner when we are done. Come with me, Shelly. I hope you don't mind the stairs. The office is on the third floor, and this is part of my exercise program."

"Not at all, I take the stairs and walk whenever possible," Shelly said, knowing she didn't if there was an alternative. Once in the AUA office, she hoped there would be a few minutes for her to catch her breath before she and Evelyn began their meeting.

"There's tea, coffee, or water if you like."

Shelly followed her into the break room, the two of them small-talking about Shelly's trip to this point, answering Evelyn's question about how she knew Joyce Chitepo.

"I don't know her. A mutual friend who knew I was coming to the UK, hoping to meet people such as you, said he would talk to Joyce to see if she knew anyone who might be interested in seeing me. I appreciated the offer, but honestly, I never expected this would result in a meeting so quickly. Thank you again for your time, Miss Walker."

"You're welcome, Shelly, and please call me Evelyn. Follow me, we'll be more comfortable talking in my office."

Once there, Evelyn motioned for Shelly to sit on a couch while she sat in a chair directly across from her.

"I believe this is a combination holiday/looking for a job trip for you, isn't it?

"Yes, but with more emphasis on the job rather than a holiday. And just to be more open about it, I intend to immigrate to the UK. That will be much more likely to happen if I have a position viewed as essential to the company hiring me. One, they cannot easily fill with local applicants."

"A skilled worker visa; I know it well. With that, you can work in the UK for up to 5 years, at which time you can apply for settled status. If granted, that will allow you to apply for British citizenship. There is more to it than that, but that is the path I believe you want to follow. Tell me more about yourself; did you happen to bring your CV with you?"

"I did," Shelly said, reaching into her purse for a copy for Evelyn. "What would you like to know?"

"Let me take a moment to review it. I did when Joyce faxed a copy, but I would like to go over it again."

Shelly sat quietly, hoping not to appear nervous as Evelyn reviewed her CV. A few minutes, seemingly more to Shelly, passed before either of them spoke.

"It is no coincidence I was available to meet with you so soon after you arrived yesterday. Based on what your friend told Joyce about you, which she told me during a phone conversation soon after, I thought there was a strong possibility you are who we are looking to hire. We've just met. I want to introduce you to one other person, but I need to know a lot more to be sure. That said, based on your CV and meeting you now, I am very impressed."

Shelly was shocked to hear this. She thought she might have a courtesy meeting, and now learns there is a strong possibility she will be offered a job.

"Ms. Walker," Evelyn corrected her, "Please, call me Evelyn, Shelly; we are very familiar here at AUA."

"I apologize; you did tell me that. I am overwhelmed by all you have said. While I had some hope this would be more than just an introduction meeting, I did not expect you to have something specific in mind. Something that might help me with my immigration status. Thank you!"

"I understand, Shelly. I believe in being very candid with employment applicants, particularly for positions like the one we are considering for you. Please be the same with me in return. Would you like to know more about what we are thinking?"

"I would, please continue."

"The position, based here in Bristol, is Africa Business Development Manager, reporting to our Africa Manager. It requires extensive travel throughout Africa, primarily in the southern and northern parts of the continent, and in central Africa in the future, as those governments stabilize. As you know better than I, many are too unstable now to expect much business for what we do. Your role would be to travel to countries where we have a reasonable expectation of increasing our revenue from tourist packages. You would meet with managers of hospitality services, such as hotels, restaurants, in-country travel agencies, tours, etc. Tell them who we are and why working with us will benefit them. Some of our competitors do something like this, and we have as well. However, as far as we know, none of them, including us in the past, has done this in person. That would be you. What do you think so far?"

Not wanting to appear overly excited, Shelly attempted to answer in a measured way.

"I need to hear more to say with certainty I can do what you expect. However, knowing only what you've told me, I believe I can. What else can you tell me about the position, compensation, and other benefits aside? No point getting into that until we both believe I am the right candidate. And may I ask a few questions, the answers to which will help me determine if I am the right person?"

"Certainly, Shelly; what would you like to know?"

"You need to know more about me, I understand, but what is it about me to this point that makes you think I might be the right person for this job?"

"Your age, gender, education, the fact that you are an African, check all the boxes, which is why I was looking forward to meeting you. You are here in Bristol. We've been talking; you present well, you provide thoughtful answers, and you ask the right questions. The fact that you occasionally fail to remember to call me by my first name, notwithstanding...," Evelyn paused, smiling at Shelly, who hoped the blush she felt in her face wasn't obvious, "... you appear to be, as the Americans would say, from central casting."

Shelly wasn't sure what that meant and decided to smile as though she did, hoping Evelyn would continue.

"I said the position requires extensive travel, the great majority of which, in the beginning, would be in Africa. By extensive, I mean two weeks a month, on average, the balance of time here in the office working with your team members who will create programs you will use to benefit clients. What do you think about that? Be honest, it's a lot of time away from home. It will no doubt interfere with any personal relations you have or expect to have. A lot of time in hotels, on airplanes, eating in restaurants by yourself. I'm older than you; I know I couldn't do it."

"You say you couldn't do it, you're older than me. Being honest, which you said you wanted me to be, I can see you are older, five or six years older..."

Evelyn interrupted her, laughing, "Shelly, you know I am every bit of ten years older than you, maybe more. But thank you for the compliment, however calculated it may have been."

Shelly smiled before continuing.

"Five or six years is a long time for management employment. Who knows where you will be five years from now? Or me if I am offered this job. I can do five years. I can possibly do ten years, but somewhere during that time, I hope I will be considered for a different role in the company, one that requires less time away. If the company ultimately believes I am not qualified for anything other than this position, that may suggest I wasn't the right choice in the first place."

"Well said, Shelly, thank you. How long will you be in Bristol?"

"Given our discussion, as long as you consider me a potentially viable candidate."

"Good. I have another meeting starting soon. I want to discuss this with Edmund Caule, our Africa Manager. Edmund is out of the office today, but he relies on my judgment making hiring decisions. I want the two of you to meet, which could happen as soon as the day after tomorrow, when he is back in the office. Would that work for you?"

"Yes, it would, and it will give me tomorrow to be a tourist in Bristol. Just let me know the time, I will be here."

"Wonderful, Shelly, thank you for coming. I am very happy we met. Is 9 AM the day after tomorrow okay with you? As far as things to see and do in Bristol are concerned, I recommend the Brunel's SS Great Britain ship at the port, the Roman Baths, and one of my favorites, the Clifton Suspension Bridge. The area surrounding it is beautiful. And if you have time, Cabot Tower is a great place to view much of Bristol."

"Thank you, Evelyn, 9 AM the day after tomorrow, to meet Edmund will be fine. And I will try to see as much of what you suggested as possible."

The meeting concluded, Shelly left the office, finding a taxi to take her back to the hostel.

CHAPTER
TWENTY-SIX

SHELLY SPENT THE NEXT DAY EXPLORING SOME OF EVELYN'S SUGGESTIONS. By late afternoon, tired and hungry, she looked forward to an early dinner and a good night's sleep to be at her best meeting Edmund the next morning. However, not unexpectedly, she was a little anxious regarding how that would go.

Edmund is the African manager; what does that mean? What does that position do, and how does it relate to what I would do? If I report to him, shouldn't he decide who is hired? So many questions; hopefully, I will know more after we meet.

———

The next morning, Shelly arrived at AUA's reception area 15 minutes ahead of her meeting with Edmund. Evelyn came out to the lobby to greet and bring her back to the conference room.

"How did your tourist day go?" Evelyn asked as they entered the conference room, finding coffee, tea, and water waiting for them.

"Couldn't have been better; thank you for the suggestions. I didn't make it to the Roman Baths, but I did the ship, the tower, and the bridge. You were right about all that, particularly the area surrounding the bridge. Just beautiful."

"I'm happy you enjoyed it. Being honest, I had reservations about taking this job, which required me to relocate here from London. I did not know much about the area and was a little elitist about leaving London. But that changed once here. There is so much to do, and you're a relatively short train ride to Paddington when you want to visit London. Coffee, tea, water?" Evelyn said, standing up to serve Shelly, whichever she requested.

"Thank you, water would be fine. I did have a question about the Clifton Bridge, do you know..."

As she was about to ask her question, a man entered the room, smiling at Shelly.

"Shelly, let me introduce you to Edmund Caule, our Africa Manager. Edmund, this is Shelly Bennett. As I mentioned to you on the phone yesterday, we had a wonderful discussion regarding the Business Development position. She is visiting Bristol as part of a UK holiday, but took time to meet with me to discuss possible employment. I am very happy the two of you can now meet to discuss working together."

"Evelyn has said a lot of good things about you, Shelly. Thanks for coming in today on your holiday."

Edmund moved to Shelly's side of the table to shake her hand.

"My pleasure, Edmund. I am here as a tourist; however, I'm also looking for employment, hoping to immigrate to the UK. There being a position here that I am potentially suited for is a happy coincidence."

Evelyn stood up, her teacup in hand.

"I have another meeting starting shortly. I'll leave the two of you to talk, and will see you before you leave, Shelly."

"Thank you again for your time and suggestions, Evelyn."

"You're welcome. We'll talk later, Edmund." Evelyn said as she closed the conference room door behind her.

"Would you care for tea or coffee, Shelly?" Edmund asked as he poured himself a cup of coffee.

"Thank you, no, I have my water."

Edmund sat down, putting his coffee on the table in front of him.

"Evelyn gave me a detailed summary of you, along with a copy of your CV. Because of that and her enthusiasm about you, I can see why.

You must have other questions I can answer. If so, please ask whatever you like."

"Well, to start, I appreciate all the positive reinforcement you have both shown me. It's my understanding I would report to you, is that correct?"

"It is, but you would effectively be acting very independently of me. We would set goals for what you hope to accomplish, along with budgets and timing. With that complete, you're off to client meetings. We assume you will spend approximately half your time traveling throughout Africa, with most of that in the north and south, where I believe you are from, correct?"

"That's right, Zimbabwe."

"The other half, you will be in the office working with support staff and me, whose responsibility is to develop the tools you will need to do your job. There are limits to what we can do, but hopefully not to the point of compromising your efforts."

"Since I would report to you, I was a little surprised that the hiring decision would come more from Evelyn than you. I assume that if you had major doubts about me, Evelyn would not overrule you. I would not want her to, regardless. Is there a reason the hiring decision is not coming from both of you, or just you?"

"Good question, yes, there is. I requested that Evelyn make the primary decision with my input after meeting you. A major consideration for hiring anyone in a management role at AUA is whether that person will be a fit for our culture. Evelyn has been with the company far longer than I have. She knows everyone at all levels of management much better than I do. She created the culture we all want to see continue in the company. I trust her judgment to see that happens."

Shelly listened carefully, wondering if Edmund's answer was more politically correct than honest. There was no way to judge which was more likely.

"I understand. What can I tell you to help you decide whether we might work well together? It's a big step for both of us. You don't want to waste time hiring someone you later find is not a fit for you or the company. I'd be closing out my life in Zimbabwe, moving to Bristol.

There is always risk, but I want to minimize the chance of it not working for either of us."

"It is a risk, Shelly, and I wish there were some way to mitigate how large a risk it will be. I don't see any way to do that. I have great faith in Evelyn's judgment about who we hire, no matter who that person reports to. I've been here a little over a year, and I've never seen her hiring decisions fail. I liked you when I walked into this room based on your CV and what Evelyn told me. I like you even more after our short time together this morning. We need someone like you, but it is you we want, assuming you want to join us. I know you wish to be supported when you apply for permanent residency and citizenship. We will do all we can to help you with that."

Shelly looked down at her water glass when Edmund finished, thinking about all he said. She assumed the final decision was still up to Evelyn, but Edmund was signaling he hoped she would accept their offer.

"Thank you for being so honest with me. That goes a long way toward making me feel comfortable despite how fast all this is happening. Three days ago, I was a tourist in London who saw little chance of finding a position in the UK, much less one that accommodated my desire to immigrate here. I realize you and Evelyn need to decide whether I am the right person. If you both believe I am and the specifics of the offer work for me, I will be more than happy to join AUA."

"Fantastic, Shelly, that is good news. Let me see if Evelyn is available for us to talk. If she is, I am certain it will be quick, and she will want to meet with you after to discuss you joining us. If all works out as we hope it will, we do not want you to leave without a firm offer to consider. Okay with you?"

"Yes, more than ok; thank you, Edmund."

"Wait here, make yourself comfortable. I'll check with Evelyn," Edmund said as he left the conference room, closing the door behind him.

Shelly reflected on her meetings with Evelyn two days previously and today with Edmund.

In my wildest imagination, I never would have guessed something would happen so quickly. I would have missed this had I gone ahead with my plan to move to Israel.

That thought startled Shelly, leaving her with a sick feeling in the pit of her stomach.

What am I thinking? He still means something to me. We may end up together at some point. But this is happening now because it was supposed to happen. Whether or not Lionel and I will be together remains to be seen.

CHAPTER
TWENTY-SEVEN

IF YOU DON'T KNOW WHICH PATH TO FOLLOW, SHOULD YOU CHOOSE TO *follow any of them?*

That's the problem, I don't know.

Things may not turn out as you hoped, even when you choose the right path. One decision leads to another, and regardless of whether you decide to move to Israel, the UK, or to stay in Zimbabwe, all your choices could lead to the wrong result. You can never know for sure which path will be best for you. Plan your life, but be prepared to change your plan when things do not work out as you hope. You can do no more than that.

CHAPTER
TWENTY-EIGHT

WHILE VERY PLEASED WITH THE OUTCOME OF HER MEETING WITH EDMUND, Shelly quickly brought herself back to a point of neutrality regarding a possible job offer today.

If it comes, I will carefully consider what it all means. No rush to judgment, my decision will impact the rest of my life.

Less than half an hour after Edmund left to speak with Evelyn, the conference room door opened, and the two of them walked in together, smiling, sitting down across the table from Shelly.

"I apologize for keeping you waiting, Shelly. I had to finish a meeting before talking with Edmund. We have talked, and now want to let you know where we are, and to hear what you think."

Here it comes, whatever it is. Stay calm, hear them out.

"Edmund and I want you to join AUA as soon as possible. If you accept our offer, we know you will need time to wrap up your affairs at home and relocate here in Bristol. We can't do much about that other than give you the time you need. But we can help with your relocation tasks here and your expenses."

Edmund continued, passing an envelope across the table to Shelly.

"Shelly, this includes the terms of our offer. You might want to follow along as I go over the details. We wanted you to have the offer in writing, to consider over the next day or so. Assuming you accept, we will work with you to develop a timeline for joining us. Sound good?"

Shelly removed the offer paper, nodding, waiting for Edmund to proceed.

"Your annual starting salary will be £12,500. You will have an annual bonus tied to the achievement of goals we will jointly agree are fair to you and AUA. The details must be worked out, but we believe this will fall in the range of 15% to as much as 30% of your annual base salary. You will have the statutory pension, sick pay, and social benefits. Human Resources will go over the details of that when you join us, or before if you'd like that discussion to be part of your decision process. We will do all we can to help you with your relocation expenses. Not knowing exactly what that will be, I can say now it will include all transportation costs for you to fly back and forth during the relocation period and an amount to be negotiated for shipping your personal effects when you decide what you will bring with you. Finally, we will do all we can to help you with your request for permanent residency. Have no doubt about that; it is possible we want that to happen more than you do. It is in our best interest that we do so. Before I continue, do you have any questions to this point?"

Shelly struggled to contain her excitement.

"Not at this moment, but I will say the offer, as you've outlined it, is very fair. I do want to think about it before responding, but I won't take too long, a day or so at most."

"Which is exactly what Edmund and I want you to do, Shelly. We are very comfortable with you. If we weren't, we wouldn't have made the offer so quickly. But in fairness to you, you have more at stake. A new demanding job in a foreign country. Giving up your life in Zimbabwe, your friends and family so far from you here. Please take whatever time you need, continuing on holiday, to make certain what you want to do."

Evelyn's words removed all final doubt regarding Shelly's decision. She felt extremely wanted by Evelyn and Edmund. But she would take time to think about it while traveling.

"Well, Evelyn, Edmund, what can I say? You have both been so kind to me, and I want to join AUA very soon. But as you say, I do need to consider this carefully. My next stop was to be Manchester, followed by Edinburgh. I will skip Manchester and go directly to Edinburgh for a couple of days, three at most. Edinburgh and London were the two places I most wanted to visit. Relaxing there, I will have all the time I need to consider your generous offer."

"That's more than fair, Shelly. Get lots of rest, and enjoy yourself. We look forward to seeing you again on your first day of employment."

CHAPTER
TWENTY-NINE

THE MEETING OVER, SHELLY TOOK A TAXI BACK TO THE HOSTEL TO BEGIN changing her itinerary. She somewhat wished she had accepted AUA's offer immediately and would return to Zimbabwe to prepare for her move to Bristol instead of continuing to Edinburgh. But she knew that would be as hasty a decision as was the one she had almost made moving to Israel.

I will give this careful thought. I'll enjoy the rest of my holiday using the next couple of days to make certain I do the right thing.

While there was a less expensive, faster train option from Bristol to Edinburgh requiring a train change, Shelly opted for an hour-longer trip with no transfers. More time to consider how different her life would be while watching the English countryside pass by. But she did make one additional change.

No more sharing a room in hostels with people I don't know. I am an adult, I am about to start an adult job. I can afford better. And since I want to be in Old Town Edinburgh proper, the Ibis Edinburgh Centre Royal Mile Hotel in Hunter Square is perfect—the location, the photos of the rooms, even the price.

The six-hour train ride to Edinburgh was slightly longer than she expected, the result of two delays. But having left Bristol at 6:30 AM, Shelly had time to enjoy the trip and, more importantly, time to consider her job offer.

I see nothing in this that concerns me. It is more than I could have hoped for. If I still feel this way tomorrow, I will call Evelyn first thing the day after to tell her I accept.

Shelly put the offer letter in her purse, settling back in her seat to watch the view as the train continued to Edinburgh. However, given the early departure and all the stress she had experienced since arriving in London, now including whether she should accept her job offer, she was soon asleep.

———

Are you certain this is what you want?

Why wouldn't I be? The offer couldn't be better; I will accept it.

You felt something similar about your decision to join Lionel in Tel Aviv, didn't you?

I did. I was too hasty in deciding that. But I also decided not to, which is why I am now in a much better situation.

What will you do about Lionel?

I will write and tell him all that has happened. He will understand this is part of us attempting to learn if we should be together long-term. I realize it will be more difficult with him in Israel, me in Bristol half of the time, all over Africa the rest of the time. But that is what I must do, just as he had to return to his job and family in Israel.

Keep thinking about all of this, Shelly. Not so you will change your mind, but so you will not later wish you had.

CHAPTER
THIRTY

SHELLY THOROUGHLY ENJOYED HER TIME IN EDINBURGH. SHE SPENT MOST of her free day in Old Town and the surrounding area, visiting Edinburgh Castle, the underground vaults, and a graveyard tour. She would have liked to have gone on one or more of the day tours. Time for that just wasn't there this trip, but she promised herself she would come back to do all of it when she has more time.

The day ended with dinner at a local pub just off Castle Terrace on Cambridge Street, a place she picked for the ambiance rather than the food, about which she knew very little.

I like the way it looks more than I care about what I will eat. I will have plenty of time to learn about that when I move to Bristol.

Dinner complete, tired from her full day sightseeing, Shelly took a taxi back near her hotel, telling the driver to let her off anywhere in Hunter Square.

I love this place, its history. I am tired, but I have enough left in me for one early evening walk before heading back to the hotel and bed.

Back in her room, she called the front desk to request a 7 AM wake-up call to be ready to call Evelyn around 8:30 AM. She lay down on the bed to think about her day and tomorrow's call.

Do I have any doubts about the offer, working for AUA, or my relationship with Evelyn or Edmund? I need to be certain. Once I commit, there will be no turning back. And Lionel will have to accept this is what I want and need to do.

She paused, rethinking all of it, the last thought in particular.

Nothing is forever; if this doesn't work out, I will choose something different. But as of this moment, I am certain it is the right choice for me.

Trying and not entirely succeeding to convince herself she had thought through everything well enough to put aside her doubts, she looked back on her day as a tourist.

What an incredible city, and all I've seen is a portion of Old Town. I must come back to see more of Edinburgh.

———

"Yes?"

"This is the front desk calling, as you requested. It is 7 AM. The temperature today will be 22 °C. Have a pleasant day."

"Thank you."

Shelly hung up the phone and lay back, promising herself she would relax for just a few minutes more.

Before the wake-up call, I was asleep, and when I hung up, I still wanted to lie in bed a little longer. Until I remembered, I would call to accept AUA's offer. I'm looking forward to that, a good sign I've made the right decision.

Shelly dressed, and with an hour before she would call, she went down for breakfast. Now, back in her room, she dialed the phone number on Evelyn's business card, waiting for someone to answer.

"Ms. Walker's office, how may I help you?"

"This is Shelly Bennett. I believe Evelyn is expecting my call this morning," Shelly said, recalling Evelyn telling her to use her first name.

"Good morning, Shelly, let me see if she is available."

"Thank you."

Less than a minute later, the receptionist returned to the call.

"Shelly, Evelyn asked if you could wait for a few minutes. She's just completing another call."

"I will. Thank you."

Less than two minutes later, Evelyn came on the line.

"Good morning, Shelly. I did not expect to hear from you so quickly, but I am glad you've called. I hope you're enjoying your time in Edinburgh. There is so much to see and do there, and you've had so little time."

"It is an extraordinary city. I've enjoyed every minute of my time here. I thought it was best to call you early this morning, Evelyn. I know you and Edmund said you looked forward to my decision."

"We do, Shelly, and we both hope you have good news for us."

"It's certainly good news for me. I've carefully considered your offer, the position, working with Edmund, the others I haven't met, and, of course, with you, Evelyn. The offer is more than fair. I accept and look forward to starting as soon as possible."

"Oh, Shelly, that is wonderful news! Just a minute, someone just opened my door," Evelyn paused to speak to her assistant.

"Yes? Perfect, send him in. Sorry for the interruption, Shelly, my assistant just came in to say Edmund was asking if I have a few minutes for him. He just walked in. Edmund, I'm talking with Shelly. I'll put her on speakerphone. Shelly, please repeat what you just told me."

"Good morning, Edmund, how are you?"

"I'm fine, Shelly, and I hope you are as well. You have news for us? I hope it's what I want to hear." Edmund said, sitting down opposite Evelyn.

"After much thought, I accept your offer, no changes necessary. I look forward to joining you both and meeting the others as soon as possible."

Edmund stood up from his chair, clapping his hands.

"Bloody brilliant, that is, Shelly! I look forward to you joining us. We have much planning to do. You need time to move here, but as for right now, I will savor the moment!"

"Well said, Edmund. You have made us very happy, Shelly," Evelyn added. "Please take time to organize your thoughts regarding all you must do before you arrive here. Take whatever time necessary. When you have your plan, please share it with Edmund so he can arrange a place for you to stay while you look for something permanent. The two of you can also begin to plan your initial tasks once you are here."

"Thank you both. I understand the details of what I will do are still to be decided. That's to be expected, given how little time we've had to discuss me joining you. The majority of my decision comes down to feeling very good about the two of you. I know I've made the right decision."

"Thank you, Shelly. Edmund is nodding in agreement. We feel the same about you. What is your immediate plan now?"

"My next call is to the airline to arrange a flight back to Zimbabwe. I checked this morning, and that is possible from Edinburgh. But it is cheaper with fewer stops leaving from London. I will most likely take the train back to London and fly home from there, coach, of course."

Evelyn immediately spoke up.

"We didn't think to mention this in your offer letter. Let the airline know you work for AUA. Since you are not currently on our employee list, they will check with us, and we will verify that you are now an employee. We will notify all airlines from which we receive ticket discounts, along with the hotels you will stay at while traveling on business. And Shelly, book business class whenever you fly on our behalf, including your trip back to Zimbabwe. You will be flying so often, you do not have to fly coach if business class is an option."

"Oh my goodness!" Shelly exclaimed. "I never assumed or even thought that might be part of the position. Thank you both so much."

"You are welcome, Shelly, and we are grateful you have accepted our offer. Is there anything more we can help you with today? Edmund, do you know of anything? He's shaking his head."

"No, Evelyn, Edmund, again, thank you both. I will fax you my timing for the move, Edmund, once I'm back in Harare. Goodbye to you both."

"Travel safe, Shelly, and I will watch for your fax. We look forward to seeing you soon."

Shelly hung up the phone, jumped up from her chair, dancing around the room.

"I-CAN'T-BELIEVE-THIS-JUST-KEEPS-GETTING-BETTER!   The

perfect job, the salary, everything. I fly BUSINESS CLASS? Really? First things first, change my flight home leaving from London. I have to make a list of what I must do when there, how much time it will take, and when I will arrive back in Bristol."

CHAPTER
THIRTY-ONE

SHELLY SLEPT MOST OF THE FLIGHT FROM LONDON TO HARARE, IN PART because she was so relaxed after what turned out to be an abbreviated holiday, pleased with her decision to accept AUA's employment offer, and this being her first time flying business class. She quickly made her way through customs to the area where friends and family waited for arrivals. Eve was there waiting for her.

"Shelly!" Eve called out, waving to get her attention. Shelly walked quickly to her. They embraced, and Eve immediately made the greeting a one-sided conversation.

"I'm so happy to see you. I got your message. I don't understand what you are doing. We have so much to talk about. Let me help you with your luggage, my car is nearby." Eve said excitedly as she took one of Shelly's suitcases from her.

"It is so good to see you, too, Eve. Thank you for picking me up. I am sorry for what was a very confusing message. I will explain it all to you on the way back to my apartment."

"Confusing? That's an understatement. More like, 'What the hell are you doing now?'"

Shelly laughed as they reached the car. The luggage loaded, Eve turned to Shelly sitting beside her in the car, speaking in a very solemn tone.

"I am not joking, Shelly, start at the beginning and explain everything. You went to the UK on holiday. You meet someone from Israel, and after only a day or so, the two of you decide you will be together for the rest of your lives IN ISRAEL! You then decide, no, that isn't what you want to do, you will continue on holiday alone. You accept a job offer, one that requires you to move to Bristol. Confusing? Are you kidding me?"

At this point, while she did not want to, out of concern for Eve's feelings, Shelly laughed uncontrollably. Eve was right; it made little sense to someone who didn't know the rest of the story. And even after hearing what the rest of the story was, Shelly doubted it would make much sense to Eve, regardless.

Finally able to stop laughing, Shelly responded.

"Eve, you know my UK trip was always more than just a holiday. I want to immigrate to a country where I prefer to live. One that is not Zimbabwe. I understand you are comfortable here regardless of what type of government we have. I am not. I love you dearly, Eve, but I have to find somewhere else to live my life. I cannot stay here."

Eve started the car and began to drive, her attention on the road ahead as she replied.

"I understand all that, Shelly. What I do *not* understand is how quickly, little more than a week, you went from moving to Israel to be with the love of your life, someone you had only known a few days, to deciding that was not what you would do. Instead, you find a job in a foreign country away from everything and everyone you know. Doesn't that sound a little strange to you?" Eve said, momentarily taking her eyes off the road to look directly at Shelly.

Realizing that Eve was very serious, bordering on angry, Shelly adopted a more serious tone for her response.

"On the surface, it does sound strange, maybe even crazy. I will tell you more, but I doubt you will feel differently when you hear the rest of it. I didn't look for a job as much as one fell into my lap. A person I know knew I was interested in finding something elsewhere, particularly in the UK. He knew enough about me to ask a contact of his to reach out to someone in Bristol, including sending that person my CV. I was told to call her when I arrived in Bristol. I did. The woman, the CEO of the company, met with me the next morning. That went very well, and she asked me to come back two days later to meet the manager I would be reporting to. I did, and that also went well. They offered me the job in writing, telling me to continue my holiday while considering their offer. They said to take as much time as I needed, but it was clear they were looking for an answer as soon as possible. I continued to Edinburgh, thinking about everything. It is the right choice for me, Eve. I probably can't make you see that, but it is. I accepted their offer and will move there in the next few weeks."

Eve did not respond, just continued driving, looking ahead. A couple of minutes passed, and Shelly could stand the silence no longer.

"Eve, I apologize for laughing. That was just my nerves knowing what I've done and will now do would not make sense to most others, certainly you included. I value our friendship. I want us to continue being friends. My new job requires extensive travel throughout North and South Africa, including Zimbabwe. I look forward to seeing you every chance I get. Please don't be angry with me."

Eve turned her head toward Shelly, her expression more relaxed. She paused for a moment before looking back at the road ahead.

"Well, Shelly, you're doing it. I can see that you are. I hope it all works out as you plan. We are friends, and I love you too. I hope you come back to Zimbabwe more often than you will probably want to. Here's your apartment; let me help you get your luggage inside. I'm sure you are tired, but how about having dinner with me tonight? My treat."

"Oh, thank you so much, Eve. We will always be friends. Yes, let's have dinner, but since you took me to and picked me up from the airport, and because I'm the one with a new job *and* an expense account," Shelly said this last part with a look she hoped Eve would interpret as playful, "I insist on paying. You pick the place, a special place, and we will have a great evening with many more to follow."

CHAPTER
THIRTY-TWO

I CAN'T BELIEVE I'VE ACCOMPLISHED SO MUCH IN JUST 10 DAYS. TAKE CARE *of a couple of small details, book my flight back to Bristol. I should be there in a week at most.*

Have you done all the important things?

I have most of it; there are only a few still to consider.

What about Lionel? Is he less important?

Shelly paused, knowing she hadn't written him, had not spent much time thinking about him other than occasionally reminding herself she needed to tell him how her plans had changed.

No, I haven't, but I will soon. I just don't know what to say.

Isn't what you will say what you are about to do? And if so, are you putting it off because less than three weeks ago, you told him something quite different? Is it because you no longer see him as part of a life you could choose to live with him if you wished to do so? There is no in-between in this, Shelly. Do not forget you are visiting alternative lives you could have lived had you not committed suicide. Doing so was your choice. Had you not done that, had you made different choices, you could be living one of these alternative lives. You are blessed or cursed, depending on how you choose to look at it, because you have what most people will never have. The chance to pick your immortal existence in a universe parallel to the one in which you ended your mortal life. Lionel is expecting to hear from you in one of your alternative immortal lives.

You are about to begin another, which may have nothing to do with him. What will you do?

Shelly hadn't thought much about her new reality. Or rather, she chose to ignore it. She only did so when her immortal subconscious forced her to acknowledge that her mortal life was over. She was now visiting lives she could have chosen to live, one of which included Lionel.

What does this mean? I cannot return to mortal life, that no longer exists. I can only briefly experience what some of those alternative lives would have been. One, if I move to be with Lionel in Tel Aviv, the other if I move to Bristol. Will we continue to communicate, one day deciding to be together somewhere?

Yes, those are two possibilities, along with an infinite number of others with and without Lionel, in countless places other than Israel, Bristol, and Zimbabwe. Remember, Shelly, every choice you could have made would have led you to an alternative existence. Your mortal life ended, and you have the option to visit a very small number of immortal existences. I said option for a reason. Not choosing is a choice, one that will place you in an eternal existence in a parallel universe not of your choosing. What do you want to do?

For the first time, Shelly completely understood the finality of her mortal life, along with the ability to have some say in what her immortal life would become.

CHAPTER
THIRTY-THREE

Dear Lionel,

I don't know where or how to begin this letter. I only know I must do so now.

No matter what you think about what I say, I want you to know I care for you greatly. Please believe me.

We agreed when we parted in London that we would soon be together in Tel Aviv, to ensure we both wanted to be with each other for the rest of our lives. That is what I wanted. I believe it was, and may still be, what you wanted. As true as that was, my circumstances have changed.

After you left, I stayed on in the UK with my first stop after London being Bristol. The details of what happened there are unimportant, but the result is, I was offered what appears to be the perfect job for me in every respect. I have accepted the offer and will move to Bristol in the next couple of weeks.

You know I came to the UK on holiday, also hoping to find a position that would enable me to obtain permanent residency, and later, citizenship. We didn't discuss it much, but that was my intent until I met you. We, and I feel it was mostly me, all too quickly created a plan that might put us together, hopefully for the rest of our lives. I know we said it was all about a trial relationship, but speaking for myself, and I'm not proud of this, I saw little or no possibility that things would not work out for us. I should have. And here's something even worse. I still feel that way. So why am I now telling you my plans have changed?

For reasons I can't explain to myself, not to mention to you, I believe we might still be together at some point. It could turn out that way. However, very little of everything wrong with what we've experienced in our short time together, including me telling you I have changed my direction once again, is not my fault. I could say we can still remotely test our relationship, that my accepting a job over 3,000 miles and countless travel hours apart will work. It might, but I don't believe it will. I owe it to myself, and more importantly, to you, to tell you that now.

I will end this as I began it. I care very much for you, Lionel. I won't say this is the end of a relationship we barely began. I've reached too many conclusions far too quickly to do that again. Time will tell.

I wish you the best life possible, Lionel. I hope to somehow stay connected with you, if only as friends.

Love,

Shelly

SHELLY FINISHED ALL SHE NEEDED TO DO IN HARARE. DISPOSING OF WHAT she would not take with her, providing Edmund with a summary of her moving plans, saying goodbye to friends, all enabled her to move as soon as possible. Throughout all this, she thought about her letter to Lionel.

A week since I mailed it, surely he's read it by now. I don't know if I will send him another with my return address. Am I cutting ties with him altogether? Why can't I be certain about this?

————

The day of her trip to Bristol arrived. Shelly had taken Eve to dinner the night before after repeatedly turning down her offer to take her to the airport.

I can't go through that again, nor do I want to make it so hard on Eve. We will see each other. I promised I would when I come back on business. Best now for me to go!

Edmund faxed Shelly, telling her he had a reservation for her at the Bristol Royal Hotel, within walking distance of Bristol's Old Town, a location he was sure she would enjoy. Lots of restaurants, pubs, things to see and do, and a short taxi ride to the office. He would meet her plane to help her with her luggage, taking her to the hotel. They would discuss things she may not have thought about, such as where she might want to move to permanently, whether she would want a car, which would require her to get a UK driver's license, a Citizen Card for identification purposes if she did not, and so many other things one new to a city and country would need to consider.

With all this and the challenge of leaving her life behind in Zimbabwe, Shelly, now seated comfortably in business class, looked forward to her new life and her new job in Bristol.

———

The flight went well, and while Shelly fell asleep shortly after take-off, she quickly awoke, her mind racing with anxious thoughts, starting with Edmund meeting her at the airport.

That is very kind of him, but I almost wish he wouldn't be there when I arrive. I'm tired. I won't look my best. However, at least I won't have to figure out how to get to the hotel with my luggage.

Once through immigration and customs, Shelly walked through the arrival exit, almost immediately finding Edmund in the crowd of those meeting passengers coming off their flights.

"You made it. I'm so glad to see you. I've been worried your flight might have arrived early and you wouldn't have any way of letting me know. How was your trip?"

"Excellent. It's so nice of the company to allow me to fly business class. That makes such a difference. And thank you, Edmund, for arranging everything for me, the hotel, and meeting me here, particularly on a Sunday. I hope I've not upset plans with you and your family."

"You haven't. My mother, father, and sister all live a couple of hours away. I wouldn't have seen them today anyway. And it wouldn't be right to leave you to find your way to the hotel on your own, regardless. Not a problem, happy to help you. Thank you for sending me your thoughts and questions about your new position. Well put together, we have much to talk about. But first, my car is in the lot outside; let's get you to the hotel and settled."

On the drive to the hotel, Edmund commented on places she might like to see and things to do during her time off. But, he was quick to add, there might not be much personal time until she became acclimated to her new position and fellow staff members.

"Shelly, if you think Evelyn and I were in a hurry to have you join us, you're right. We are very happy you're here. But we didn't throw the first person we met into the job. We interviewed three others, all UK citizens with limited to no knowledge of or experience in Africa. We knew that when we brought them in for an interview, based on their CVs. But they looked good for other reasons; you looked even better. You checked all the boxes. I know, so American, I love saying it." Edmund said, smiling, before continuing. "But it was your interview that convinced us you are the right person. And the more exposure we have to you, the more certain we are that hiring you is the right thing for us."

Shelly laughed, "I don't know how American saying all the boxes are checked is. I'm not an American, but I have said it myself. I'm glad you talked with others. It felt as though you were in a hurry to find someone for the job. I'm glad you picked me, and I feel better about it knowing you did because I 'checked all the boxes'."

"Here's the hotel; I think you'll be comfortable. The building has been modernized considerably and wasn't a hotel until recently. It had been an empty, very run-down property before someone had the foresight to restore it. It is at least 125 years old. I hope I look half as good when I'm half its age."

The more Edmund talked and joked, the more Shelly realized he was not what she considered to be the stereotypical proper British male.

"Don't we all, but you have many years ahead of you until you reach that point. We both do."

"That we do. I'll get your bags while you head to the front desk to check in. The room is in your name, billed to AUA. I will join you after I park the car."

A few minutes later, Edmund found Shelly waiting for him in the lobby.

"I'm sure you are tired after such a long trip, but you do have to have dinner. It's early. Why don't you rest a bit? I'll come back to pick you up around five if that works for you. There's a place nearby I think you will like. Casual, good food and drink, we can have our first detailed conversation about how best to get you ready for tomorrow and the days to follow. Human resources will take hold of you first thing. After they are done with you, I will introduce you to two others. The team, along with me, supporting you."

"I am tired, but a nice hot bath and a short nap will take care of that. Five sounds great!"

"Wonderful. You can leave a message for me at the front desk if anything changes. If not, I will see you at five here in the lobby. Bring a coat. It's comfortable now, but it will get a little chilly after dark."

Once in her room, Shelly welcomed the time alone, although not because she didn't like Edmund. On the contrary, she was very comfortable with him, increasingly so the more time they spent together.

Being tired, Shelly almost fell asleep in the hot bath. Now, out wearing a terrycloth robe provided by the hotel, she lay down on the bed, thinking a few minutes with her eyes closed would revive her.

What is that noise? Where am I? Oh my lord, it's the phone.

Shelly sat up on the edge of the bed, quickly picking up the receiver.

"Hello!"

"Shelly, are you alright? This is Edmund."

Surprised to hear his voice, she looked at the clock near the phone to see that it was almost 5:30. She had overslept.

"Edmund, yes, I am alright, embarrassed, but fine. I lay down after a hot bath for just a few minutes. That was over two hours ago. I am so sorry."

Edmund laughed, "Long plane rides followed by a hot bath and just a few minutes of quiet lying on a comfortable bed will do that to a person. I hope you feel better. Are we still on for dinner?"

"Yes, certainly, and I am hungry. Can you give me half an hour to pull myself together? I don't think dinner in my hotel terrycloth robe would be acceptable. You might uncheck one or more of those boxes you mentioned."

Edmund laughed again, "No, you're probably right, you would certainly be testing the restaurant's dress code. Take whatever time you need. I'll wait for you in the lobby."

Shelly quickly opened her still-packed suitcase, looking for something to wear. She dressed and went to the bathroom mirror to fix her hair.

"I won't make the best impression, but this will have to do."

Twenty-five minutes later, she came off the elevator in the lobby, walking to Edmund, sitting in a chair, reading a newspaper.

"Well, haven't you broken some unwritten women's rule about not only *not* arriving on time, but arriving early?"

"Yes, two rules. One, arriving early, not late, to the revised time, while two, doing so purposely to hopefully make up for being almost an hour late from the original time."

"Shelly, I must tell you, I was very happy with you joining the company. But our initial time together did not show me your wonderful sense of humor. That is a great quality for everyone. One more box checked. Now, if you are hungry, let's do something about that."

"Thank you. I am hungry, I'll follow you."

"The restaurant is a little further than I remembered, so we will take my car. Another one-hundred-year-old refurbished building, I think you'll enjoy."

CHAPTER
THIRTY-FIVE

SHELLY WAS IMPRESSED WITH THE RESTAURANT BOTH OUTSIDE AND INSIDE. Looking around as they were escorted to their table, she commented.

"I have not seen much of the world. I know there are beautiful old buildings in many countries, but I am struck by how many I have seen in my brief time in Bristol. London, I expected and found them. I had no expectations for Bristol, but it's true here as well. Evelyn gave me some great suggestions for my one-day sightseeing around the city. I saw many, and this is another one."

"You're right about that. A great meal is always preferred, but having one in a building such as this makes it even more special. I assumed Bristol would be a step backward from London in all respects. It's not. I never tire of exploring Bristol and the surrounding areas. Your challenge will be deciding what to see and do in what order. I can help you with that if you like.

"You have already, Edmund. I couldn't imagine a better welcome than you've given me today."

Their conversation over a drink before dinner and with a bottle of wine during dinner resulted in both being more spontaneous. They didn't talk as much about Shelly's new position as she had assumed they would. It was more about each of them personally. Neither of them was or had been married and were not seeing anyone now. Shelly did not mention Lionel.

At one point, the conversation slowed, with each looking in a different direction. Hoping to break the awkward silence, Shelly looked at Edmund and spoke.

"You look as though you are thinking some very deep thoughts. Would you care to share whatever that is with me?"

Slightly embarrassed, Edmund looked at Shelly, then down at the table.

"I guess I did get a little distracted. I didn't know it was that obvious."

"It wasn't, not in a bad way. You just appeared to be drifting. I wasn't offended; you've devoted your entire Sunday to me, how could I be?

"I wasn't thinking of something else. It just hit me how often things turn out very differently from what we expect. Less than a month ago, Evelyn and I were uncertain how we would ever find the right person for your position. Then, seemingly out of nowhere, you appear. We didn't find you; you found us, and just at the right time. Life's funny, isn't it? We plan, things change, we make new plans, and in the end, we don't know if what is, is better than what might have been."

These last few words startled Shelly. She didn't know why, just something about what he said made her think they were more than a random thought.

"Edmund, where did that come from?"

"What? What I said?" He paused, his head turning slightly to the left, looking away from Shelly. "Good question, I don't know. I suppose I was still thinking about how we planned to fill your position, and then there you are."

"I understand, but what you said sounded very familiar to me, although I don't know why. I thought you may have picked it up from some business conference."

"I may have, but if so, I don't recall from where. But it is true, isn't it? People make all sorts of plans, some of which work, some don't. And when a plan does work, we can't be certain that the outcome was as good as it would have been had we done something else."

"It sounds as though you're having second thoughts about hiring me."

"Oh, God, no, Shelly, absolutely not! Whatever I was thinking had nothing to do with business or you joining us. I apologize if you thought otherwise.

What Edmund didn't say was that it had *everything* to do with Shelly.

"I think we may have overstayed our welcome here. It looks like they would like us to leave. And you must be exhausted. I'll drive you back to the hotel."

"I am tired but not exhausted. It's been a wonderful day, this dinner, this place. Thank you for all you've done for me today."

"My pleasure, believe me, and here's another thought. Instead of you taking a taxi to the office tomorrow, I will pick you up at your hotel at 8:30. You can ride with me to work."

"Oh no, Edmund, you don't need to do that, you've done so much for me already. I can get a taxi to the office."

"I know you can, but I want to start your first full day off properly. Eight-thirty, ok?"

"Eight-thirty and I promise not to oversleep. I will meet you out front."

Edmund dropped Shelly off at her hotel. Once in her room, she thought about all that had happened since he met her at the airport.

What a first day back in Bristol. I never would have guessed it would go as it did.

But something about it troubled her. She wasn't sure why or exactly what he said or did, but whatever it was played on her mind.

I appreciate everything he did for me, so what is it about him that troubles me? Or is it even him at all? Maybe it's me.

CHAPTER
THIRTY-SIX

YOU KNOW WHAT IT IS, SHELLY.

I don't understand. Tell me.

I am forcing you to recognize and focus on everything you need to know to decide which alternative life is right for you.

Why do I feel something is not right? Is it Edmund, the job? Am I now not sure that moving to Bristol was the right choice for me?

Remember, Shelly. Life can be strange. We plan, things change, we make new plans, and in the end, we don't know if what is, is better than what might have been.

CHAPTER
THIRTY-SEVEN

SHELLY SPENT HER FIRST MONTH ON THE JOB LEARNING WHAT SHE NEEDED to know before leaving on her first trip, meeting customers. Since there was more opportunity for that in North Africa, and because it required less travel time, her initial customer meetings were with two hotel managers in Casablanca, followed by three in Cairo. Those meetings now complete, back in Bristol, she would briefly meet with Evelyn to discuss how things went, followed by two days of meetings with Edmund and his staff, sharing what the customers told her they expected from AUA.

"I've been looking forward to hearing about your first trip, Shelly. Edmund said you have exceeded his expectations. I hope you feel good about things as well."

"I do, Evelyn. I was nervous ahead of the first customer meeting."

"That was in Casablanca, wasn't it?"

"Yes, with Zween 'Oteel, a smaller property, not part of a large group. I wanted something to prepare me for large group meetings. I think it went very well."

"I'm sure it did. I know you'll go over the details with Edmund and the team. You don't need to with me now. You met with five properties. Do you get an overall sense of what is most important to them?"

"I do, starting with the fact that I came to meet with them on-site. The other travel companies either contact them by phone or make no effort to learn their needs. Regardless of the size of the property, which varied considerably, they appreciate the personal contact. I've thought quite a bit about this and have a theory. Africans, in general, feel ignored by the rest of the world, particularly Western countries. I know this was certainly the case in Zimbabwe. Me, an African by birth, a woman, coming to them from a UK company, left a positive impression with them of AUA."

"Wonderful news, exactly what we hoped would happen. Is there more?"

"Yes, there is. Regardless of how they have been contacted, in one way or another, each manager said that promises were often made and not kept. They want to see follow-through." Shelly looked down at her meeting notes before continuing. "One of the Cairo property managers said, 'I'd rather you promised me nothing than tell me what you will do and then not do it.'"

Evelyn paused before responding.

"That doesn't surprise me at all; that person could have been talking about us. The major task I had when I accepted my position was to overcome our poor reputation for not following through. We promised a lot and delivered very little. You being here is half of what we've needed to do to improve our image with customers. The second half is providing concrete results after they visited with you. That is where Edmund and the team come in. Thank you, Shelly. Unless you have something more, I know you have much to do. I'll let you get to it. I look forward to what you and Edmund come up with in terms of customer deliverables."

"That is the high-level stuff. I have a lot of specific details I will share with the team, and I'm certain you will see much come from that very soon."

CHAPTER
THIRTY-EIGHT

SHELLY COMPLETED HER FIRST YEAR AT AUA WITH TIME PASSING AS though it were only a few months. She accomplished much, pleasing not only herself but Evelyn, Edmund, and those with whom she worked directly within AUA as well. And of greatest importance, the customers. AUA's African customer base increased by twenty percent, revenue by just over thirty percent, with a ten percent increase in net profit. Everything was going to plan.

As pleased as Shelly was with her job accomplishments, something else was happening that mattered to her more. She and Edmund had become close outside of work. They didn't talk about being a couple, but neither of them was seeing anyone else, and they were spending most of their weekend time together. Shelly thought their relationship might go beyond friendship, and she hoped Edmund felt the same. It was time to find out.

Shelly had visited the Roman Baths on a group tour one weekend, soon after moving to Bristol. But she wasn't about to let that stop her from going again when Edmund suggested the two of them do so a few months later. They enjoyed the trip, and now, at dinner, she felt the time had come to see what Edmund's thoughts were about them beyond work.

"I had a wonderful time today, Edmund."

"I did, too, Shelly."

"We've had a lot of good times together this past year, haven't we? I hope it continues."

"I see no reason it wouldn't, at least until you get tired of me or we run out of places to go and things to do," Edmund said, smiling.

"I don't know about things to do, but I'm not growing tired of you; in fact, quite the opposite."

Shelly looked down as she finished speaking. Edmund caught her meaning. Looking at her, he replied.

"I believe I understand, but just to be sure, are you wondering what our relationship is and where it's heading?"

Shelly was relieved she didn't have to find some way to bring up the subject.

"I am, and as you so often do, you've made what I want to ask you easier for me. We are coworkers, and I don't want to do anything that jeopardizes our ability to work together. We are also good friends who have fun together outside of work. But is there more to it than that, as far as you are concerned? I will tell you how I feel, but first, let me know what you think."

Edmund looked to the left, appearing nervous.

"I think my questions have made you uncomfortable. I apologize," Shelly said

"That's not it, I've been anticipating this discussion, looking forward to it for some time. Now that it's here, I'm not sure what to say. Well, that's not exactly true. I do, but as you said, I don't want to negatively affect our work and personal relationships."

Shelly sat upright, taking a deep breath before replying.

"Ok, it's time one of us clearly said what they're feeling. Edmund, I care a great deal for you, maybe even love you. If you don't feel the same towards me, I accept that. I know we can continue working together. I'm not sure I can continue spending as much time with you if we're just friends. I think that..."

Edmund interrupted her.

"Say no more. What you've said is what I hoped you would say. Exactly how I feel about you. I've thought a lot about us this past year. We've had these feelings for some time without compromising our work relationship. There's no reason it needs to do so in the future. I don't know where we're headed, but I'm glad we have this out in the open."

Shelly smiled at Edmund before speaking.

"Well, for two people who say they like, maybe even love each other, we certainly have put a damper on this day. Weak attempt at humor, forgive me. I feel as though a weight has been lifted off me, having said what I did, hearing your response. So, boss, where do we go from here?

Edmund laughed, "There it is again. Your humor and timing are impeccable. Here we were on cat paws with each other as though there were a pane of fragile glass between us. You smash the glass, clearing it all away. Well, I can too. We need more time together to know for certain what our relationship is and might become. I'm looking forward to experiencing that with you. But as for now, I want you to know, I love you, Shelly."

"Wow! I did not expect to hear that from you when this conversation began. I hoped you would tell me you liked me and wanted us to continue seeing each other. But love? I believe I know what you mean. If we were to part now, I would always think of you as though we had been in love. So why not say it? I love you, too, Edmund."

Shelly and Edmund continued spending as much time outside of work with each other as possible. They talked about moving in together to a new place for both of them. But they first wanted to discuss it with Evelyn to let her know how close they had become. While the company had no policy preventing personal relationships among employees, they felt it was right to assure Evelyn that their personal relationship had not negatively affected their work, nor would they allow it to do so in the future.

———

Evelyn's assistant scheduled a meeting for the three of them in the conference room. Both let her know how they felt about each other, including their plan to live together. When they were done, they asked if this was a problem for the company.

"What kind of CEO do you think I would be if I hadn't noticed how close the two of you have become? Does it concern me? It does a little, but not for the company, for both of you. Continuing to be as successful professionally as you both have been requires your full attention. And your relationship, as you've now described it, requires even more attention. Doing one or the other is very difficult. Doing both at the same time borders on impossible. I know you don't see that now, but you will in time. At some point, separately or together, both your work and away relationships will be challenged. All of that comes under the heading of advice from your work 'mom'. I would say unasked for advice, but you did ask my opinion, didn't you? That is what I think, both as your boss and your friend. Do your best to make sure your personal relationship does not negatively impact your professional relationship. If it does, and I don't see you able to deal with it, I will."

CHAPTER
THIRTY-NINE

WHILE NOT UNEXPECTED, EVELYN'S ADVICE WAS SOBERING FOR BOTH Edmund and Shelly. They knew her well enough not to be surprised.

It did cause them to be more discreet while at work. They did not talk to others about what they did on weekends. They purposely sat far apart in meetings, sometimes even disagreeing more than necessary, hoping to demonstrate to their coworkers that when it came to their jobs, they were acting independently of each other.

After spending the better part of two weekends looking at apartments, they settled on one on Manila Road just off Clifton Down. Chosen because of its proximity to parks, Clifton College, restaurants and pubs, a diverse mix of younger professionals living nearby, and finally, public transportation alternatives to Edmund's car.

The first few weekends were spent shopping for essentials for their new apartment. Both enjoyed this as much as they had their sightseeing weekends, Shelly in particular.

———

At home one evening midweek, Edmund was engrossed in a BBC documentary regarding the Vietnam War while Shelly was arranging newly purchased bedding and towels in their bedroom.

"Edmund, please come here for a moment, I want your opinion about something."

"Does it have to be this minute? I'm watching something very interesting. Why don't you join me? You can ask whatever you want during a commercial."

"I need to show you something, but I suppose so," Shelly replied, picking up two bath towels before joining Edmund in the living room.

As she walked in, he said, "Perfect timing, my show just went to a commercial. What do you want to show me?"

Shelly sat next to him on the couch, unfolding and laying the two hand towels next to each other in his lap.

"I can't decide which would look best in the loo when we have friends over. What do you think?"

Edmund laughed, "That is a difficult decision for you, is it?"

"Well, I want it to look right. Why are you laughing at me?"

"I'm not laughing at you, Shelly, more with you. And while we're on the subject, it's funny hearing you use the word "loo" with your Zimbabwe accent."

"Would you prefer I call it a gezi? I would were I back in Harare," Shelly said, playfully hitting Edmund with one of the towels.

"I suppose not. You pick whichever is best, using the second one on other occasions. Don't be angry, my show is starting again. Why don't you take a break and watch with me? It's very interesting. Sad, but interesting seeing what those American boys are going through."

The documentary resumed, and as Edmund suggested, Shelly stayed to watch some of it with him, listening to the narrator describe the scene.

"Not wanting to appear as though they intended to change North Vietnam's government, the Americans limited their ground fighting to South Vietnam. This allowed the North Vietnamese to bring supplies into South Vietnam through southern Laos almost unabated. The North Vietnamese and their allies, the South Vietnamese Vietcong, often enjoy the advantage of surprise given their extensive knowledge of trails and terrain throughout South Vietnam."

"One example of this was a battle that occurred on the first of August

1970. The US Army Echo Company, 508th Infantry Battalion, 101st Airborne Division, was ordered to an area bordering a mountain as a backstop should the enemy facing their A and B sister companies, believed to be on the opposite side of the mountain, attempt to retreat west. However, unknown to US intelligence, A and B companies were confronted by only one of the three regiments; the remaining two had already moved west two days earlier. Echo company had unknowingly stumbled into and was attacked by the remaining two NVA regiments. Over three thousand well-equipped NVA soldiers against one hundred seventy-five 101st Airborne soldiers. The issue was never in doubt. Echo company suffered over seventy-five percent killed and wounded casualties."

Shelly instantly stood up from the couch.

"I can't watch this, I *can't!*"

On the verge of crying, she ran from the living room to the bedroom, shutting the door behind her.

Completely shocked, Edmund turned off the TV and went to the bedroom, where he found Shelly on the bed, lying on her side. He sat down next to her, placing his hand on her shoulder. Her body was rigid, her breathing rapid and deep.

"Shelly, what's the matter? Are you ok?"

She didn't answer, continuing to breathe deeply as though she wouldn't be able to breathe at all if she didn't.

"Shelly, please tell me, what's the matter? Can I get you something?"

She slowly turned on her back, looking up at him, appearing as though she wanted to speak but was having difficulty doing so.

"I can't...I can't watch that show, Edmund, I can't! There are others about the war I have seen. I watched them, but not this one."

"I'm so sorry, I had no idea it would affect you this way. If I had, I never would have suggested you watch it with me.

Beginning to relax somewhat, her breathing slowly returning to normal, Shelly responded.

"It's not your fault. I don't know why, there is something about this one that..." She paused mid-sentence, saying no more.

Edmund lay next to her, his closeness relaxing Shelly. A half-hour passed, and still unable to say why she reacted as she did, they decided to get ready for bed and, hopefully, a good night's sleep. The lights were out, both still awake, and Shelly brought it up again.

"Something about that battle, the description of it, frightened me terribly. I don't know why. I have no connection to it. But it's almost as though I did. I've never felt that way about any war, including that in my own country. Why this one?"

"I know, Shelly. It's best to put it out of your mind. Try to sleep."

He leaned over to kiss her goodnight. She didn't resist or respond, just continued looking up toward the ceiling as though answers to her questions would be there.

"Goodnight, Shelly, I love you."

CHAPTER
FORTY

EDMUND AWOKE THE NEXT MORNING NOT AS REFRESHED AS HE WOULD have liked. He knew Shelly had not slept well, tossing and turning most of the night. He decided not to ask how she felt out of fear that would rekindle whatever caused her so much discomfort before bed. Both were now ready to leave for the office. Shelly looked and sounded tired, nothing like most mornings before last night.

"I know we said we'd try the bus today, let's do that some other time. I'm a little tired and don't want to deal with it. I'll drive us to the office," Edmund said, hoping Shelly would think this was what he wanted, not because of her.

He had been looking forward to trying public transportation to and from work. It seemed very convenient, much less expensive than driving, maybe quicker, given dedicated bus lanes. But not today. Shelly still appeared to be thinking about last night's documentary, and not in a good way. She responded.

"Whatever you say, I'll be ready in five minutes."

Based on her lethargic response, Edmund knew Shelly was not doing well.

"Are you okay going to work today? I'm concerned about you. Maybe you'd be better off resting at home."

Without looking at him or even turning in his direction, Shelly quietly responded as she put on a sweater and reached for her purse and briefcase.

"No, I'm fine, just a little tired. I'm ok, let's go, we don't want to get bogged down in traffic."

She started toward the door, Edmund following. While the temperature had been comfortably warmer over the past week, today, there was a chill in the air. Shelly shivered as she got into the car.

"I am a little cold, please put on the heat."

Edmund did as she asked and started their drive to the office. There was no conversation between them during the twenty-minute ride. Edmund thought how unusual that was, how much Shelly typically had to say during their daily commutes. With few exceptions, always in a good mood. Today stood out in stark contrast to all previous days.

———

Walking from the car to the office, Edmund thought about his schedule.

We're fortunate we have no meetings together today. It's better if I'm not around her, possibly reminding her of last night.

Once inside the building, they immediately went to their separate offices. No embracing or even a few moments of conversation, as other employees would sometimes do before beginning work. Edmund knew today was different, as though there was now an unseen barrier between the two of them. One he hoped would not be there on the way home.

Shelly's schedule included a three-hour review meeting with staff working on support material for her trip beginning next Monday. Nothing unusual, the typical conversation about upcoming meetings with potential and existing clients, the material she would present to them, and some discussion about unexpected things that might come up along the way. True to her reputation, Shelly fully concentrated throughout it all. None of the team saw any behavior different from her past behavior.

The day over, Edmund waited for Shelly at the door to the parking lot and their ride home. She smiled as she approached him.

"My Monday review meeting ran over, but for good reason. We had much to discuss regarding the Horizon Hotel presentation. Not quite there yet, but close. How was your day?" Shelly said as she and Edmund walked to the car. He was pleased she seemed much more like her usual self.

"My day? Easier than yours. I'd like to say I miss those review sessions, but honestly, I don't. And you do a much better job than I did covering all the details. I forgot Horizon was on the agenda. How's that looking?"

"I'll know for certain a week from tomorrow when the meeting is over. But the prep feels about where it should be with time to push it all the way before I head out."

———

The ride home went well enough, although not as good as most days. Shelly generally had more to say than she did this afternoon. However, she was more engaged than she had been during the ride to work. Not perfect, but much improved.

They worked their way through a simple dinner at home, including a glass of wine. Edmund thought that might relax her as they finished cleaning the kitchen. Whatever it was, he welcomed Shelly, bringing up the previous evening.

"I want to apologize to you for last night and this morning. I know I've not been myself. It is not because of you. Maybe I made you responsible for whatever caused me to go to such a dark place because I am so close to you. Because I knew you would let me get away with it. I have no excuses; it wasn't you. I'm very sorry, Edmund. You didn't deserve that."

Shelly finished what she had to say while continuing to dry and put away the dishes. Edmund rinsed and dried the last few pieces of silverware before responding.

"It was a side of you I've never seen. I was scared seeing you so frightened. And you were such a different person on the way to work this morning. I was very happy to find you largely back to normal on the way home. There's no need to apologize, Shelly. I know you weren't placing the blame for whatever happened to you just on me."

He put the towel down and walked the few steps to her in their small kitchen, reaching out to hug her. She accepted his embrace.

"I don't know when or even if I will ever completely forget last night. It frightens me, not knowing what scared me as much as it did. But I will not let that come between us. I love you."

"I love you, too, Shelly."

The rest of their evening was spent watching TV, with no connection to Vietnam, before going to bed to read. Around 9 PM, they put their books down, kissed goodnight, and slept soundly.

CHAPTER
FORTY-ONE

THE MONTHS FOLLOWING THEIR FIRST REAL RELATIONSHIP TEST WENT WELL, personally and professionally. Shelly, Edmund, and the support staff continued to enjoy great success, with sales and profits increasing significantly. Shelly and Edmund were happy, Evelyn was happy, and if she had any complaints or reservations about their personal and work relationships, she kept them to herself.

Shelly traveled every bit as much as Evelyn said she would. At first, it all being new, she enjoyed it. But as the months passed, the initial excitement had passed, and she focused more on the impact it had and would have on her personal life. She and Edmund decided they did not want to marry. They saw themselves as a successful couple, very much in love with each other, with no need to be married. They were committed to each other, even more so than many married couples they knew, certainly more than those who had since divorced. Recently, they decided they would add to their family. Shelly stopped taking birth control medication, and much sooner than expected, she learned she was pregnant.

———

"Edmund, we need to talk. We agreed we wanted to start a family, but it never occurred to me how soon that would happen."

"What are you saying, Shelly? Are you...you're pregnant?"

"Yes, I am! The doctor just called with the results of yesterday's test. I am *definitely* pregnant. She wants me to come in for a thorough exam. When I do, we'll know how far along I am. But there is no doubt *I am pregnant.*"

Neither of them said anything more, just looked at each other, processing what this meant, not the least of which was what it meant to Shelly's travel schedule. Well before deciding she would stop taking birth control, they talked about the impact her pregnancy would have on her career. They were proud of having thoroughly weighed the pros and cons of having a baby before deciding that it was what they would do. But now that it was reality...

"Edmund, what will we do? I never dreamed this would happen so quickly. It's hardly been a month since we decided to try to get pregnant, and now I am! *Try*, Edmund, not *be* pregnant, at least not this soon!"

Edmund laughed, but seeing Shelly so animated, he kept his thoughts to himself.

Cool, calm, collected Shelly is losing it.

"It has come sooner than I thought it would. But this is what you wanted, isn't it? I mean, if it weren't now, it soon would be. We'll adjust. You continue to work until you're no longer comfortable flying or when the doctor says you must stop, whichever comes first. We now need to meet with Evelyn to discuss her plans for your position. We owe her as much lead time as possible to reach a decision. We'll do that tomorrow, agreed?"

"Yes, you are right, we have to. I just hope she'll have options allowing me to keep working without having to travel so much."

———

The next morning, Shelly asked Brittany, Evelyn's assistant, for a time the three of them could meet to discuss Shelly's position in the company. Brittany asked if that was the subject, and, unable to think of anything else, Shelly said it was.

"You told Brittany the meeting was to discuss *your position in the company*? You're kidding?" Edmund responded when Shelly told him their soon-to-be meeting with Evelyn was scheduled.

"I did, I couldn't think of anything else. You don't think Brittany or Evelyn will know what that means, do you?"

"Oh, no, of course not, how could they? Shelly, you might as well have said we wanted to discuss your baby shower! Brittany knows, she will gossip with her friends; she probably already has."

Edmund was only half serious about Shelly having let slip what they both hoped would stay with Evelyn, at least until it was clear to everyone that Shelly was going to have a baby. The other half he found to be funny.

"So, what time do we meet? I hope it's this morning before the entire company knows."

"It is. Brittany put us down for 10 AM, another forty minutes or so."

"Ok, then, we might as well make it official."

Five minutes to ten, Shelly and Edmund walked past Brittany into the conference room to wait for Evelyn. Once inside, the door shut, Shelly asked, "Did you see how Brittany smiled at me? She knows."

"Oh, come on, Mom, you new mothers are always so suspicious," Edmund said, winking at Shelly. She was about to tell him this was no laughing matter when the door opened, and Evelyn entered, moving to the opposite side of the table, smiling at them as she sat down.

"Brittany put this meeting on my calendar, citing that the purpose was to talk about your position in the company, Shelly. Is there something either of you would like to tell me, or should I guess? Wait, don't tell me. I want to guess. Congratulations to you both! When are you due?"

Speechless, Shelly could not answer, a look of total surprise on her face. Edmund smiled broadly.

"We're not sure what the due date is. My guess is around eight months from now, give or take a few days. We will have a better idea after Shelly meets with her obstetrician next Tuesday. Thank you for congratulating us, Evelyn. I don't know how surprised you are, but we certainly were. I mean, we had agreed to try but did not expect results so soon."

Evelyn laughed, standing up, her hand outstretched toward them.

"I hadn't expected it, no pun intended, until I saw Brittany's meeting note. But I do congratulate you both and assume that besides wanting me to know, you also want to discuss your responsibilities, Shelly, correct?"

"Yes, that is why we wanted to meet, Evelyn. Thank you for congratulating us. We want to give you as much time as possible to decide how to transition my travel schedule to someone else. You told me when you offered me the job that the day would come when I could no longer travel as much as required. I understood what you meant. But it never occurred to me that the reason would be because I was pregnant."

"I'm sure you didn't, but pregnancy was one of the possibilities I had in mind. So you are, and now we must decide what to do. Do either of you have any thoughts?"

Shelly and Edmund briefly looked at each other, unsure who would speak first. Shelly began.

"Whatever the plan, if possible, I would like to continue working in some role not requiring extensive travel. Edmund and I have not discussed how much time we will need away after the baby is born. We also haven't talked about whether I will continue to work or stay home as the primary caregiver for the baby. Again, this has all come much sooner than we assumed it would."

"Edmund, do you have any thoughts?"

"I do, Evelyn, although just preliminary, and just about the travel part. Before I say what that is," he turned to Shelly, "we need to talk about whether you will return to work after maternity leave or decide to stay home with the baby full time. Not this minute, but very soon. Your position has to be filled by someone, and I have an idea who that might be. But the question is, will you want to return to your old job after a reasonable maternity absence? If you do, is that even possible with a baby if you continue traveling as you have to this point? Speaking as the soon-to-be father and your co-worker, I don't believe it is."

Evelyn interrupted, "I can see this has you both more surprised than I realized. Let's stop here. The two of you decide what you want to do. When you have, we can get back to plan B."

"Yes, thank you, Evelyn. We certainly need more time to consider life after the baby is here. We will talk about it and bring you back into the discussion in the next day or so."

The meeting over, Evelyn hugged both Shelly and Edmund, wishing them the best of luck.

"I support you both and will do all I can to make this work to the satisfaction of all of us. Thank you for sharing your news with me today, and again, congratulations to you both."

SHELLY'S AND EDMUND'S CONVERSATION ON THE DRIVE HOME THAT NIGHT and the next morning was all about what Shelly wanted, including what would be best for the baby.

"I want to work, I enjoy it, but I am ready to give up the travel, at least as much as I have been doing."

"I'm glad to hear that. The baby notwithstanding, I am ready for you to be home more than you have been. So I assume you are saying you want to come back to work after a reasonable maternity absence."

"Yes, maybe six weeks at most. If my new position, whatever that might be, pays enough to justify it, I would like to find a daytime nanny to be with the baby. However, I may need to take a cut in salary and bonus. That could amount to quite a reduction, so much so that it would not pay for me to work. If that is the case, and you agree, I will stay home full-time to care for the baby. You need to think about that, too, Edmund. It affects *our* income, not just mine, and the baby's care."

"You're right, and I have been thinking about it. Can we proceed assuming there will be a position that pays enough to justify a nanny we are willing to trust with our baby? If so, and you like the position you are offered, is that our plan B? You will come back to work after six weeks, give or take."

"Agreed with one modification. I can decide whether I want to continue staying home with the baby at the end of the maternity leave, rather than now or when it begins. I can't say I will be okay leaving the baby in someone else's care, no matter how capable they may be. My maternity instincts may overrule that."

"I understand. I don't know if we can conclude anything more now. What we do is dependent on how we feel when the baby comes. We just have to live the experience to know what is best for the three of us and AUA."

The conversation stopped at this point, with both of them pleased with how quickly their plan came together. They hoped they would feel the same before meeting with Evelyn in a day or so.

"Ok, Shelly, how about what will soon be your last opportunity for a celebratory glass of cabernet for the next year and a half? I included breastfeeding in that timeline." Edmund said, smiling.

"You pour, I must conserve my strength," Shelly replied, winking at Edmund.

———

Three days had passed since their initial meeting with Evelyn, two days since they created what they hoped Evelyn would find to be an acceptable plan B. They presented their thoughts, and Evelyn responded.

"On the surface, that seems reasonable. As a mother myself, I know you can't know how you will feel entrusting your baby to someone else until that moment arrives. Do either of you have any suggestions about how to fill your current position, Shelly, as well as what you would do if you do come back?"

Edmund responded quickly.

"I do, Evelyn. As for the travel part, Carol is ready and capable of assuming Shelly's current position. In fact, if we don't find a growth position for her, she might move on. She has the personality necessary to meet with all levels of management. She is a 'sponge' when it comes to detail, as Shelly has been, and will bring back actionable information. I don't consider her to be a compromise. As for who will handle her duties as team leader, Shelly will tell you what we're thinking."

"Before you do, Shelly, I have a question about Carol. Does she know? Does the team know you're pregnant?"

"I can't say for certain, we haven't told anyone. But you know how rumors spread. If not now, they soon will as I get further along."

"More questions. Has Carol expressed interest in what you do? I mean, more than just thinking about how glamorous traveling is. Would she want to do this job if it became available? Does she realize how intense the travel requirement is?"

"She's never referred to my travel being glamorous or anything close to that. She asks a lot of questions about what I bring back, the meetings I have with clients, and other relevant topics that someone interested in this job should ask. As I told you when I was interviewing, this position probably has a three to five-year turnover, either for reasons similar to mine or simple burnout. I admit, after three-plus years, that has been on my mind more than in the past. I've been very impressed with Carol's ability to act on the information I bring back, creating the material I need to do my job. I think she would be an excellent choice."

"And what about you? Do you see anything you might like to do?"

"The first thing is for me to decide now whether I want to return to my old job, including all the travel, after a one or two-month maternity absence. If I did, we'd have to tell Carol that her taking over for me is only for a couple of months at most. Hearing that, would she want to accept the job? I wouldn't. It's in the best interest of the company and Carol for me to decide now. It's time for someone else to do my job, Evelyn, and I believe Carol is the right choice."

Edmund interrupted, "Let me take it from here, Shelly."

"Evelyn, we agreed we needed someone regularly traveling to meet customers at least two weeks a month. Hence, we found Shelly. I can cover her travel for six to eight weeks while she is home with the baby, and still handle my responsibilities in the office when I'm not traveling. Carol has come a long way and could fill in for me when I'm not here. If Shelly and I believe she can return full-time after maternity leave, we hope there will be a position for her. The question then is, doing what? Shelly, back to you."

"We switch roles. Carol takes my job, I assume hers. We've worked so closely. I know what she does; I can do that. And if that means a cut in salary, at least a reasonable one," she said, smiling at Evelyn, "I accept that too."

Evelyn sat back, fiddling with her pen while thinking about all that Shelly and Edmund had to say. After a brief pause, she responded.

"Thank you both very much. It is clear you've given this a lot of thought. I appreciate you being willing to accept a reduced salary should that be necessary, Shelly. It shows your willingness to support the company. Let me think about this and talk with HR. I will get back to you both in a day or so with questions and/or a decision."

CHAPTER
FORTY-THREE

EVELYN TOOK MORE TIME GETTING BACK TO EDMUND AND SHELLY THAN she assumed would be necessary. She apologized, telling them HR needed time to review the position descriptions for Shelly and Carol, salaries in particular. That now complete, and after speaking with Carol, the two of them exchanging positions was approved, effective in two weeks.

The balance of time until Shelly would go on maternity leave would be used for each to coach the other. Carol would also accompany Shelly on a couple of trips to be introduced to clients. She would receive a salary increase commensurate with her new responsibilities. Shelly will remain at her current salary, partly in recognition of her excellent performance to this point, and her willingness to accept a salary reduction if requested.

As they often did, Edmund and Shelly used the time driving home to discuss the news they received from Evelyn earlier in the day.

"I don't know how things could have worked out better for me and Carol."

"For me as well, Shelly, but we now must be doubly aware of our interaction in team meetings. We generally did anyway, but from this day forward, even more so. I'm concerned that Franklin and/or Susan might be a little miffed, having not been considered for your job or now for the team leader position. Watch for signs of that; there may yet be blowback."

"I know, and I somewhat believe they have a right to feel that way."

"Team leader, maybe, your job, no. Neither of them has had enough experience to interface with customers, nor the personality required for that part of the job. I wish it were otherwise, but that's not the case. Evelyn asked me how promotable each of them is as part of her review of you and Carol swapping jobs. You are now part of the team, and just as I would not share what I said to her with the others, I won't with you either. But I will say Evelyn agreed with my analysis. She also said she would not have agreed for you and Carol to swap positions unless she were convinced it would work." Edmund turned to look at Shelly, a neutral expression on his face, before finishing the thought. "I wouldn't have either."

"Well, thank you, sweetheart, I love you too," Shelly replied, smiling, hoping she sounded playfully sarcastic as she intended.

CHAPTER
FORTY-FOUR

THE TIME BETWEEN THE CHANGES BEING ANNOUNCED TO THE TEAM AND the rest of the company, and Shelly going on maternity leave just days before she expected to deliver, passed very quickly for Edmund and Shelly. They reasoned it was because they were so busy moving to a larger two-bedroom apartment, one a little closer to the office, preparing for their baby's arrival, and so Shelly could become accustomed to her new role in the company.

Franklin and Susan showed no signs of being upset with the change that did not include them. Carol immediately produced almost as effectively as Shelly, and all agreed it was only a matter of time before she did equally well.

Edmund was very happy with how things turned out, and while Shelly said she was too, privately, something bothered her. She couldn't say for certain what it was and wouldn't tell Edmund if she knew. Not yet, anyway. She just wasn't as happy as she assumed she would be, no longer needing to travel as much, taking up a new role in the company at her previous salary, and with a baby due any day.

What else do I want? I'm healthy, and all indications are the baby is too. Work is going well. Edmund is happy. Why am I not at least as much and possibly more so than he is?"

———

It was decided that Shelly would start her maternity leave a week before her due date, which, her doctor assured her, was the correct date, plus or minus a day or two at most. She spent the remaining time resting, attending to final details in the baby's room. Each morning, Edmund left for the office, reminding her to call if she even suspected her delivery time was imminent.

Shelly wondered how all that was about to happen would affect her and Edmund. She mostly passed it off as what any prospective mother would be thinking. However, increasingly, she thought it might be more than that.

"Oh, God, is this it?" Shelly said out loud as though there were others in the apartment who would hear her. "Why couldn't this happen when Edmund is home? Oh, there it is again. Alright, he said to call even if I wasn't certain."

She picked up the phone and dialed the office.

"Brittany, this is Shelly. Please put me through to Edmund, and if he doesn't pick up, please go look for him." She paused while Brittany responded.

"Yes, Brittany, I think this may be it. Please hurry."

A few seconds later, she was relieved to hear Edmund's voice.

"Shelly, is it time?"

"You said to call, I'm not sure, but yes, I think it is. I'm feeling sharp pains every few minutes. Can you come home now?"

"Absolutely, stay calm; I'll be there in half an hour or less."

Shelly hung up, looking around the room for something to distract her while waiting for Edmund.

Laughing at herself, she thought, *I suppose everyone is right about me. I must always be doing something I consider to be productive, or I'm not happy.*

Edmund got Shelly to the hospital with little time to spare. Less than two hours after she called the office asking him to come home, she delivered a healthy baby boy. She had no problems with the delivery, and she and the baby were discharged two days later. Now home, Shelly and Edmund knew for certain their lives had changed forever.

"Baby Carl is so good, I almost feel as though we are missing something most parents get to experience," Shelly said while breastfeeding him.

"Yes, we are, but I can do without what new parents at work have told me about their new babies. Constant crying, difficulty sleeping, not accepting breast milk; is some or all of that what you're missing?"

Shelly laughed both at what Edmund said and how silly she knew she sounded.

"Ok, you're right, we can miss that part while enjoying the rest."

"I would say you can rest now that Carl is here. However, as good as he is so far, I know we will have some rough times in the coming months. I'll do what I can to help you however possible, Shelly."

"I know you will. I love you, we will make it work."

As is true for most new parents with newborns, time passed both quickly and slowly for Shelly and Edmund, depending on Carl. They assumed he was progressing normally, crying when he needed something, rather than simply crying. Most nights, Shelly got up to feed and change him during the week, with Edmund taking over on weekends so Shelly could rest and sleep better.

Nonetheless, she increasingly sensed something was not as it should be. She wasn't certain but assumed it was postpartum and would pass in time. But she questioned how long it would last and what if it were something else?

CHAPTER
FORTY-FIVE

SHELLY, INSTEAD OF LOOKING FOR A DIAGNOSIS OR ASSIGNING ONE COMMON *to many women, open your mind to other possibilities. You committed suicide because you prematurely concluded you could no longer handle life as you were living it. What if you were to do that in this unlived life? Remember, this is only one you would have lived had you made different choices. There are an infinite number of others. If you use the same decision process in all of them, why would you expect a different outcome?*

I'm unhappy; it must have to do with giving birth.

Maybe, but what if it's not? You have questioned something else that may be causing your discomfort. Is that no longer a possibility? I am you, Shelly. I force you to consider your deepest thoughts, no matter how uncomfortable that makes you feel. Might there be something else bothering you?

Is this the unlived life I choose to live?

Is it? Life's funny, isn't it? We plan, things change, we make new plans, and in the end, we don't know if what is, is better than what might have been. Life can *be funny, but I don't believe you think your life is now. Do you?*

I don't. Edmund and I plan everything, but little of it turns out as we had hoped. What's the point?

Is that true, Shelly? Don't give up.

CHAPTER
FORTY-SIX

EDMUND, SHELLY, AND BABY CARL SETTLED INTO A ROUTINE OF EDMUND being a father, husband, and a senior AUA employee, Shelly a mom and wife, and Carl just being what most babies approaching their one-year birthdays are: a baby. Edmund didn't give this much thought. He was happy, while sometimes struggling to achieve work/life balance, managing the professional and personal demands on his time, never completely succeeding in both. The personal part was not lost on Shelly.

I knew having a baby would change things. I'm not sure I like what that has become, at least for me. I'm having trouble justifying how much of my unhappiness has to do with Edmund. I agreed and wanted to have a baby. Carl is here now. I love him dearly, Edmund, too.

Thinking this, she paused.

Do I? Do I love Edmund as I did before Carl was born? Did I ever really love him?

Shelly was having this internal conversation with herself more frequently. When the six-week mark of her maternity leave came and went, and she could not bring herself to return to work, she thought it was just a matter of having more time at home with Carl. Edmund agreed Evelyn did too, and now, with Carl's one-year birthday approaching, Shelly questioned whether her happiness was simply a matter of whether or not she went back to work full-time.

———

"Carl will be one year old in three weeks. That is the time I assured you and Evelyn that I would go back to work. But now that it's getting close, I don't know if I can."

"You don't know if you can or if you want to? Shelly, what's wrong? I understand you may have been dealing with postpartum issues. I thought that would all be resolved by now, but it looks as though it's not. Is there something more to it, something you should discuss with me?"

Maybe it was what he said or the way he said it that caused a wave of anger to wash over her. But even as it did, even before responding, she knew he had a point. There was something more. She paused to control her emotions; she did not want to lash out in anger.

"I don't know, Edmund, but I do know I am not happy. I love Carl; he is such a dear. Of course, I want to spend as much time as possible with him. But at the same time, I enjoyed working and believed I would again."

Edmund noticed she did not say she loved him.

"Evelyn has been more than patient with us, Shelly. I don't think she believes my work suffers without you there, but she might. I do. I have covered for you as best I can and have been helped by Franklin and Susan stepping up, but..."

Shelly cut him off mid-sentence, her anger unmistakable.

"You 'covered for me'? Oh, how good of you, Edmund. I didn't know there was anything about me being on maternity leave, taking care of our child, that required you to make excuses for my absence. That is what you mean by excuses, isn't it?"

"Shelly, that's not what I meant, and you know it."

"Ok, just a minute, don't say anything more; I want to finish telling you how I'm feeling. In two words, not good! I'm home all day, not you. I'm the one getting up with Carl at night, almost every weeknight. I know you help on weekends, but do not trivialize what I do. I don't know why I'm feeling as I am, but do not for a minute decide it is post-partum or something else you consider to be inconsequential."

Shelly paused before continuing. Edmund, sensing more to come, didn't say anything.

"You won't like hearing this, I don't like saying it, but it's time to bring everything out in the open. I'm glad we never married. Had we done so, if we are now at a crossroads, that would be one more thing we'd have to deal with. I think the problem is us, Edmund, you, and me. I used to be happy with you. I don't feel that way as much anymore. I sometimes think going back to work would be the answer. If it is, I cannot imagine us working as closely as we have in the past, or even both of us at AUA. I love Carl and would not give him up for anything. But I do not feel the same about us, about you."

Edmund listened to everything Shelly said, staring at her intently. When she stopped talking, neither of them said anything before Edmund responded in a quiet, measured tone.

"I could say I am shocked to hear this, but I'm not. If a man told me his wife said the same to him, I would tell him she doesn't mean it. It's just the new baby, maybe the pressure of wanting to be with her child, *and* wanting to go back to work. It could be that with you, but I've thought otherwise for some time now, Shelly. We both know the answer, don't we?"

CHAPTER
FORTY-SEVEN

EDMUND ASKED YOU A QUESTION, SHELLY. ANSWER IT. YOU WILL KNOW *when it is time to leave a place, person, or situation.*

Is that it? Do I need to leave this unlived life? I desperately want to find where I belong, as you call it, what my immortal life will be. This felt like it was that place and person. I wanted it to be, but it's not.

If you are certain it isn't, what must you do?

I must move on to whatever is next for me.

———

Am I dreaming?

What pulls me to a place I never imagined I would go? What reason am I doing so now, and what do I expect to find there? Claire thinks I'm crazy for doing this. She never heard anything more from her soldier. She just put his memory aside and moved on. Why can't I do the same? If this is a dream, please make it stop.

It is no dream, Shelly. Everything you need to know to make sense of your mortal life, and now to help determine what your immortal existence will be, you know. Accept that you do, follow your instincts, and you will find what you are looking for. Don't do that, and you will experience an unlived immortal life not of your choosing.

CHAPTER
FORTY-EIGHT

SHELLY LOOKED OUT THE AIRPLANE WINDOW, SEEING NOTHING IN THE dark, starless night somewhere over Africa, on her way to the first of three stops and her final destination, Seattle, Washington. A nine-thousand-mile, day-and-a-half journey to a city and country as far removed from her life as anything she could have imagined. One minute relaxed, the next near uncontrollable panic, Shelly contemplated what she had done, along with what lay ahead.

Why am I doing this? He won't be there; he's most likely dead. If he's not, where do I look for him? All I know about him is what little he said in his letters. I shouldn't have held on to them. I should have known things would never work out for us when he failed to meet me in Singapore.

This last thought forced her to confront what she increasingly feared to be the truth.

He wanted to come, he said so more than once in his letters. He didn't because he is dead.

The hours passed slowly. Most of the passengers were asleep, their overhead lights off. Looking around, Shelly could see that only her light was on; she was the only one who appeared to be awake. Sleep was not possible as she struggled thinking about what she would do once in Seattle. She pulled the single dog tag she wore around her neck out from her blouse, looking at it in the dim light. Raymond's name and serial number stamped in metal. She wondered where he might be, possibly wearing the second one, assuming he was still alive.

Finally, on the last flight segment from Los Angeles to Seattle, she fell asleep until the pilot announced they were beginning their descent to SeaTac Airport. Exhausted, having been awake for over thirty hours, the flight attendant struggled to wake her.

"Excuse me, miss, time to wake up; we're on final approach. Miss?"

Not getting a response, she gently shook her forearm until Shelly woke up, looking around, startled, then at the flight attendant.

"I'm sorry I had to wake you; you were sleeping so soundly. We'll be landing shortly. I need you to stow your bag under the seat in front of you."

The flight attendant continued checking passengers behind Shelly. She moved her bag as requested and looked out the window, seeing the area surrounding downtown Seattle passing below. Soon, she saw tall buildings, many more than she expected, including a tall 'needle' looking tower. Off to the left, a large inland body of water. Everything was so green, unlike what she had imagined. So beautiful. All this after the long, arduous trip flying over continents and hundreds of millions of people she didn't know and would never meet, she once again thought about the reason for her trip.

It may be foolish. No, there is no doubt about it; it is foolish. But I have to do this. I cannot continue living if I don't. If he is down there somewhere, I will do my best to find him. What happens then only God knows. And if I don't find him, that, too, is God's will. But I will have tried my best with what little time and money I have.

Shelly's tourist visa was good for up to six months, a time far exceeding the duration of her money. Assuming she wanted to stay longer than her finances would last, knowing her tourist visa did not allow her to work in the US, she nonetheless planned to look for a job with an employer who did not question her legal status. If she did find one and were caught, she would be deported, not allowed to reenter the country for a long time, possibly forever. Shelly knew all this but still considered the risk worth taking.

I have traveled before without a specific plan, but nothing like this. I have to look for him. This will likely require more time and money than I have. I don't care. I will do everything possible to either find him or convince myself I never will. What happens after that, I cannot say. I will accept the consequences.

Having retrieved her luggage, Shelly found her way to a bus an information person in the airport said would bring her close to the hostel she had booked for her stay. Near Rainier Beach, quite a distance from downtown Seattle, Shelly selected it because it was less expensive, and for another reason.

I will be less likely to have my legal status questioned by immigration authorities the less time I spend in downtown Seattle. And with no other reason for starting my search elsewhere, Rainier Beach is as good a location as any to begin looking.

Once on the bus, Shelly showed the driver the street address for the hostel.

"That's not a very nice area. Are you sure that's where you want to get off?

"Yes, if that's as close to the address you can get me."

"It is. I just wanted to make sure that is what you want."

A short time later, the driver stopped the bus and, using his microphone, said. "Lady asking about this stop, we're there. Please come forward to exit the bus."

Before she got off, he asked again, "This is it, look around; are you sure this is where you want to get off?"

Shelly leaned down to look outside. It was as he said it would be, but with no alternative, she nodded.

"This is the address I need to find. Are we at all close?"

"Turn right at that intersection ahead of us, Renton Avenue, walk two or three blocks. I'm not certain how many. Turn left on 54th Avenue South; you'll find it along there."

Off the bus, Shelly started walking, hoping it was just a short walk. If not, trailing a large suitcase with a smaller shoulder bag would be difficult.

As the bus driver indicated, 54th was only two blocks away, and once there, she quickly found the address she had booked before leaving home. A house, but not one that looked at all like the hostels she had stayed in previously. With no options, she went to the front door and rang the bell. A middle-aged woman opened the door.

"Can I help you?"

First looking at the woman, then attempting to look past her into the house, Shelly hesitantly replied.

"I hope so, I may be lost. My name is Shelly Bennett. I just arrived from Zimbabwe. I booked a room in what I thought was a hostel at this address."

The woman smiled, "My name is Kathrine. Friends call me Kathy. I've been expecting you. I understand this is not a hostel as you assumed it would be. I had to describe it as such to get it listed. But you are at the right place. I live here alone and have a room for you. I include breakfast, no lunch, and no dinner. You are not allowed to have visitors here. You are welcome to see the room to decide whether or not to stay," she said, opening the screen door for Shelly to enter. "The little money I get from guests helps me stay in the house I've lived in for over forty years. But it's up to you to decide. You don't have to stay if you don't want to. I will refund your deposit if you choose to go elsewhere."

With no options, Shelly hesitantly entered, leaving her luggage just inside what turned out to be a small but clean-looking living room, with furniture that appeared to have been here as long as Kathy said she had been. She followed her down the hall to the first room.

"This is it. It used to be my room. I moved further down the hall to a second bedroom to give guests more privacy. We each have our separate bathrooms. If you stay longer than you expect, we can talk about additional rent. What do you think?"

Without options and increasingly more at ease with Kathy, Shelly responded.

"This will do fine, much better than a traditional hostel." Smiling at Kathy, she continued, "And you will find I am as clean and orderly a guest as you are a host. I'll get my luggage."

"I'm sure I will, Shelly. I imagine you'll want to unpack. I know I said dinner is not included, but since you've just arrived, you're welcome to join me tonight if you'd like. I don't want you to think I'm nosy, but I am interested in where you are from and your plans while you are here. Where did you say you came from?"

"Zimbabwe, in southern Africa. You're not being nosy, and I don't mind answering your questions. If there are some things I'd rather not discuss, I'll let you know. But could I pass on dinner? Maybe we can talk tomorrow over breakfast. I've slept very little over the last almost forty hours, and what little I did was sitting up on the airplane. I'd just like to shower and go to bed."

"Certainly, of course, I understand. We will get to know each other at breakfast. Sleep well," Kathy said, closing the door behind her.

———

Shelly quickly put her clothes in the dresser, showered, put on her pajamas, and got in bed.

"Oh, this feels so wonderful. I hope I sleep through the night."

That was the last thought she had before going into a deep sleep."

———

Do you remember? Roosevelt High School.

CHAPTER
FORTY-NINE

"SHELLY?"

Hearing no sounds indicating she was awake, Kathy knocked a second time, a little louder and longer.

"Shelly, are you awake? It's after 11 AM; you've slept more than twenty hours. You must be starved."

Initially, Shelly thought she was back in Zimbabwe. Then, hearing what she knew to be someone knocking on a door, she began to awaken, not entirely sure where she was. She opened her eyes, looking around the room, realizing she was in Kathy's house.

"Yes, Kathy, I'm awake."

"I'd be happy to make you bacon and eggs; you must eat something. Do you drink coffee? I also have hot or cold tea or milk if you prefer."

"Thank you, Kathy. I'll finish dressing and be out in a few minutes. Please don't go to any trouble; whatever you have will be fine for me. I do drink hot coffee and/or tea, whichever is easiest for you. Thank you."

"Take your time," Kathy said as she walked toward the kitchen.

Shelly got out of bed, quickly dressed, fixed her hair, and left her room to join Kathy in the kitchen.

"There you are. I hope you slept well. You look rested."

"I did. I hardly recall getting into bed, and once there, I was immediately asleep. Oh, that smells delicious!" Shelly said. The smell of bacon rising from the pan made her hungrier than when she awoke.

"Glad to hear it. I debated waking you, but I knew you would be hungry. How do you like your eggs?"

"Let's see, I heard this is how you say in America. Is it sun up?"

Kathy laughed, "If it is, I don't know how to cook them that way. Maybe you mean sunny side up?"

"Yes, that's it. I love all the little phrases Americans have for so many things. Sunny side up. I'll remember that."

Having slept so long, Shelly was well-rested. She thoroughly enjoyed her three eggs and bacon late morning breakfast as Kathy sat with her, drinking coffee.

"I would have waited for you, but I'm an early riser, always hungry when I get up. I had my breakfast a couple of hours ago. I enjoy watching you eat so well after a good, long sleep."

Shelly finished everything on her plate, savoring her coffee as the two sat and talked. She wasn't certain how much she wanted to share about why she was here.

What would I say? I was communicating with a US soldier in Vietnam. He was supposed to meet me in Singapore on his R&R. I went; he didn't. I knew he was from Seattle, but nothing more about him. It's been close to five years since I last heard from or about him. He may be dead for all I know. I'm here to find out. Makes me sound crazy. The less I say, the better.

"Zimbabwe! I believe I've heard the name, but I couldn't tell you where it is. Are you here on vacation? Why Seattle?"

"That's a long story. The short version is, I was corresponding with a friend who lives here, or did live here. We lost connection with each other. I wanted to see some of America, so I thought, why not start by looking for him in Seattle?'

Shelly liked her answer. Less is more.

"Where in Seattle do you think he might be? This is not a big city, at least not by US standards. But you need to have some idea where to look."

"I know, and I don't have much to go on, but I believe he said he went to Roosevelt High School or something like that with 'Roosevelt' in the name. Do you know anything about that?"

Kathy stood at the sink, her back to Shelly. Hearing Roosevelt High, she quickly turned to face her.

"Do I? There's only one Roosevelt High in greater Seattle. Do I know about it? I guess I do. I went there myself, but only for a year before my parents bought this house. We moved here well before your friend was there. What else do you know about him?"

"Unfortunately, not much." Without having consciously decided to, Shelly told Kathy more of the story.

"He is, probably was by now, a US soldier in Vietnam during the war. My girlfriend was writing a friend of his, also a soldier, and suggested I write his friend. I did, he answered back, and we became friends. He mentioned Roosevelt High in one of his letters. And now you confirm there is a Roosevelt High School here in Seattle. That is wonderful news, a place for me to start."

"Not much to go on, but you're right; knowing the high school he might have graduated from is a start. I'd be happy to take you there if you like. I'm not sure they will share school records or any information about students. We could explain why you're looking for him; maybe they will help in some way."

"Kathy, that is very kind of you. I know this sounds crazy, but it is something I have to do. He was so good answering my letters. He asked me to meet him in Singapore while he was away from the war. I went, but he didn't come. I've not heard anything more from or about him since. My girlfriend's soldier friend stopped writing her about the same time. One or both of them could be dead or happily living somewhere. I don't want to interfere with that. I would just like to know what happened to him for closure's sake."

Close to tears, Shelly knew she had said way more than she intended. Kathy was very surprised and saw the pain in Shelly's face.

"Shelly, I am so sorry to hear this. I know you are hurting; anyone would be. I don't know how much I can help you, but I am happy you are with me now. I will do whatever I can to help you find what there is to know. Is there anything more you remember? Where he might have grown up, any mention of the house he lived in, possibly his friends?"

"Thank you, Kathy. I'm glad I've met you as well. Once off the plane, alone with little money or time to look for him, I was very scared. Now, just being here with you in your house, almost by accident, convinces me I am doing the right thing. I wish I knew more, but that's all there is. Roosevelt High School and his name, Raymond Quinn."

CHAPTER
FIFTY

KATHY DROVE SHELLY TO ROOSEVELT HIGH, AND AS EXPECTED, THE school's administration said they could not provide any information about students past or present. Now sitting in Kathy's car in the school parking lot, each wondered, what now?

Shelly spoke first.

"I was so optimistic when you offered to drive me here. I know I shouldn't have been, and I fully understand the school's position. But I just wanted it to work. As you were driving, I looked around, thinking how big Seattle is. What would I do if we didn't learn something more about him from the school? Where would I look next? Who might know something that would help?"

Kathy looked forward in the distance as if expecting to find something that would lead them to where they should go next.

"How long did you plan to stay before either finding him, learning something about him, or giving up? What then?"

"I don't know, I didn't think things through enough to know what I would do. What if I learned he was happily married, maybe with kids? What if he wasn't married, surprised I had looked for, not to mention, found him? What if he preferred I hadn't? What if I learned he was killed in the war? More than anything, I just want closure. I need it, Kathy! I can't continue to live not knowing."

These last seven words, spoken with unmistakable desperation, scared Kathy.

"Shelly, what do you mean you can't continue to live? What are you planning to do, assuming you don't find him or anything about him? I want to help you. I will do all I can. But I will not be a part of your self-destruction if that is what you have in mind. I have my own baggage I carry in life. I can't imagine many who don't. You obviously do. But that's no reason to do something you cannot take back."

Shelly thought that something more than accidental circumstances had brought the two of them together. Enough so that before a full 24-hour day had begun and ended, one she mostly slept through, Shelly shared far more about why she was in Seattle than she ever imagined doing with anyone. And now this person, whom she knew so little about, knew so much about her. Time to pull back. Shelly turned to face Kathy, still looking at her.

"Oh, no, Kathy, nothing like that. I am sorry I gave you that impression. It's just that so much has happened to me since I left home, and now my optimism has reached an unreasonable high only to be brought back to reality..." Shelly paused before continuing, hoping and failing to control the emotion she knew was pouring out of her. "This is all a shock to me. But I'm ok, I'll be ok, no matter what happens, including nothing at all. Believe me."

"I hope so, Shelly, I do. I promised I would help you however possible, but do me a favor, will you?"

"Certainly, Kathy, whatever I can, I will. What is it?"

"If you do decide to kill yourself, don't be anywhere near me or my home when you do."

Kathy looked out the windshield to the school parking lot in front of them before starting the car and driving off. Neither said anything during the ride back to Kathy's house, each lost in their thoughts, recalling events of the day. Shelly's mind was a blur of confusion. She told Kathy she was "ok," knowing she was not. Panic gripped her.

CHAPTER
FIFTY-ONE

HOW CAN I HAVE SO LITTLE SELF-CONTROL? WHY DO I DO AND SAY SUCH *rash things? What am I doing halfway around the world searching for someone I hardly knew, now dragging Kathy, whom I know even less about, into my messy life?*

You are right; why do you do these things, Shelly?

I don't know!

And what now? Are you giving up your search after much less than a week?

I had little to go on, now nothing, and this city is far too large to simply guess where to look. I have no idea. . .

You needn't say more. I will finish the thought for you. You are rash; you killed yourself because you are. You are now given a chance to correct that mistake, that FATAL mistake. You are blessed, and yet you continue to reach important conclusions in all too short a time with little to no information. To this point, reaching and acting on the wrong conclusions.

Slow down, Shelly. You have all the time in this world and the next to find where you want to be.

CHAPTER
FIFTY-TWO

GETTING CLOSE TO HOME, SHELLY SPOKE THE FIRST WORDS EITHER OF THEM had since leaving the high school.

"Kathy, I apologize if I have upset you. I know everything I am doing, along with much I have said in the short time we've been together, will make little sense to you. It doesn't always to me, either. But I am slowly pulling things together. I used the wrong words today. If you had said the same to me, I would have reacted as you did. I apologize. I am not going to kill myself around you or anyone else. I need to slow down, to take things as they come."

She paused before continuing, before Kathy could reply.

"If there is somewhere reasonably close to your home where I can get some dinner, please let me off there. I'll eat and walk home after. I feel the need to do both."

"Apology unnecessary and accepted. I understand the enormous pressure you are under. I could never have done what you are doing, no matter my age. Will you accept some advice from a woman with more years behind her than ahead?"

"Yes, please."

"You have no chance of creating a plan to accomplish all you wish to do on this trip by yourself. You are off to a good start. You are here. You have been to the high school from which your friend graduated. It was unlikely you would learn anything about him there, and you have now confirmed that is the case. You did choose the wrong words today, but would you ever really consider killing yourself after doing so little to discover what you want to know? If you would, you might as well have stayed in Zimbabwe, ending your life there."

Kathy paused before continuing.

"I do know a place close by for dinner. I will take you there on one condition. I join you. We've both been through a lot today, and I don't want to eat at home by myself."

"Certainly, Kathy, I appreciate the company. My treat."

"No good, Shelly, Dutch treat, and if you don't know what that means, I'll explain it to you at dinner."

Twenty minutes later, they arrived at Collier's overlooking Lake Washington. Close enough to Kathy's home by car, too far for Shelly to have walked home had she not been with Kathy. They went inside and were soon seated at a window table overlooking the lake.

Shelly quickly looked at the menu, a concerned expression on her face. Seeing this, Kathy spoke.

"Do you know what Dutch treat means?'

Shelly shook her head.

"It means we each pay for our own. I don't know how long your money will last on this trip; it's not my business to know. We've had a difficult day. I don't go out like this often, and I would appreciate you letting me pay tonight."

Shelly put the menu down before responding.

"Thank you, Kathy, you've already done so much for me. I can afford what I would like to have for dinner tonight. But since I will be with you for a while, and because you already know something about why I am here, probably more than you would know about most of your guests, let me tell you about my money situation. I am here on a six-month tourist visa. I booked your home for four, possibly six weeks. I had no idea how much time I would need to accomplish what I came to do, maybe less, maybe more. I still don't know. If I needed more time, I planned to look for a job where I wouldn't be questioned about my legal status. I don't even know if such jobs exist. But I did research it enough to know that quite a few people from other countries do that once they are in the US. I would, too, if after a month or so I found good reason to keep looking. If not, I would return to Zimbabwe."

"I know people do that. I've read stories about companies being raided, illegal workers being arrested. Are you aware that the punishment includes the workers being sent back to their home country, in many cases, banished from reentering the US for five years or more?"

"I am."

"And you are willing to accept that risk?"

"Under the right circumstances, yes."

"No promises, Shelly, but I know of something that might work for you. I assume the rest you might choose to tell me has to do with what you do or don't find out about your friend, correct?"

"Yes, it is."

"Let's save that for our breakfast conversation tomorrow, ok? This view, this food deserves our full attention."

Shelly agreed, they ordered dinner and a glass of wine, while looking out over the lake as twilight fell over the water.

Up to this point, Kathy asked more questions about Shelly than Shelly asked about Kathy. Shelly decided to balance their conversation.

"I believed when I arrived, you said you had lived in your house for forty years. Is that so?"

"I have, first as a teenager when my folks purchased it, and later when I inherited it after they passed. I was sad when we moved after my freshman year at Roosevelt. But I quickly settled into my new high school and made new friends. I have mixed feelings about still being here, among the ghosts of my parents," she said, looking around the room before continuing, "but I know I wouldn't be happy living elsewhere."

"Do you mind my asking, were you ever married or living with someone?"

"I don't mind. Yes, I married at far too young an age, both my husband and I. We lasted a little over two years before correcting our mistake. We divorced twenty-five years ago."

"Do you regret any of the choices you've made that have led you to where you are today?"

"I do, and anyone thinking about their lives should as well if they are being honest about themselves. That is a problem for all of us. But we more often think about what we got wrong, not enough about what we did that was right. I know that's certainly been true of me. How about you?"

Surprised by what Kathy said, Shelly looked out across the water, thinking before responding.

What I've done right. Do I think about that enough? Do I think about it at all?

"Do I think enough or at all about what I've done right? To answer your question, no, I focus more on my failures than my successes. I do my best to put what didn't work behind me. It happened; best not to think about it. But that is easier said than done. And as far as my successes are concerned, there's little of that *to* think about."

"Are you sure there is no value in what you regret? Is there no good in failing? You should give yourself credit for what you do right, but there is also value in examining what you did wrong. Take me as an example. My failed marriage was not solely the fault of my ex or me. I've thought about it a lot. I see what each of us should have done differently, starting with *not* having married so quickly, so young. I was too naive; I lived in a dream world. I didn't think about how we would both change when the 'honeymoon' period was over. I could list what my ex should and should not have done, but that would not be fair to him. What he needed to do only he could identify for himself. We all must self-assess, hopefully improving our chances for success in life by not repeating past mistakes."

Shelly realized her self-assessment was always one-sided. Her focus was on what she did wrong, never considering what she did right, never analyzing her mistakes, hoping to learn from them rather than just self-criticizing.

"I said I have something in mind for you. A job that may financially enable you to stay longer, should you choose to do so. Let's head home and discuss that tomorrow at breakfast, along with your search plan."

Once home, Shelly went to her room, showered, and to bed.

I shouldn't feel as good as I do about how things turned out at the high school today. Kathy told me to think about my failures to learn from them.

What can I learn from today? Kathy, and what she said about self-assessing. She's right, there is much more ahead of me with my search. The high school part is neither good nor bad; it's just part of the process to learn what I need to know. And I will learn even more tomorrow, and the next day, and the next. This has been a very successful day.

CHAPTER
FIFTY-THREE

SHELLY AWOKE, REFRESHED, LOOKING FORWARD TO MORE CONVERSATION with Kathy.

Maybe I slept so well because of my last thoughts before falling asleep. Self-assess successes and failures, learn from the latter, appreciating the former. I will do more of that.

She hurriedly dressed, left her room, and found Kathy standing at the stove cooking bacon as Shelly entered the kitchen.

"Oh, Kathy, that smells so good. We have something similar in Zimbabwe, we call bhekoni. But it never tasted as good as what you make."

Kathy turned around, a spatula in her hand.

"Good to see you up, you look well-rested. What did you call it, beekony? Is that the language of Zimbabwe?

"I am well rested, thanks to you. Actually, it's bhekoni in Shona, one of many languages spoken throughout Zimbabwe. I was raised speaking English. I understand a lot of what is said in Shona as long as the speaker speaks slowly. I can speak a little of it as well, but almost everyone in Harare understands and speaks English."

"Bhekoni, hmm, I'll have to remember to drop that into a conversation with my friends. They'll be impressed. I hope you're hungry. In addition to bhekoni, I'm making pancakes. Do you have that in Zimbabwe?"

"Honestly, I'm not sure, and if we do, I don't know what the Shona word would be for them. How do you make them?"

"Good question; I'm not sure. I use pancake mix I buy at the store, add a little milk, egg, stir until all the lumps are gone, and fry until golden brown. I like mine with a little maple syrup and butter. Try it, you may like it."

Oh, I will, that and the bacon..."

Kathy corrected her, "bhekoni!"

Smiling, Shelly responded, "Excuse me, you're right, pancakes and the bhekoni smell wonderful, and I am hungry."

Their breakfast over, Kathy and Shelly did the dishes before moving into the living room to have a second cup of coffee.

"Do you like children, Shelly?"

"I do very much. I have a niece and nephew back in Harare. I'm missing them more than I thought I would. More than I miss any of my friends or my sister."

"Last night, I said I had a job that may be right for you. A friend of mine who lives four doors down the street from me is looking for someone to watch her two children three days a week while she's at work. A two-year-old boy and a four-year-old girl. Good kids, I enjoy being around both of them. If that sounds like something you could do, I will introduce you to their mother."

"Knowing only what you've told me, it does sound like a good fit. Would she have a problem with my legal status?"

"I don't know, that's a detail the two of you would have to work out. I could call her, briefly explaining your situation to see if she is open to meeting you."

"Please do. There's no point in taking up her time if she is not okay hiring someone on a tourist visa. If it is a problem for her, should I be concerned that she might report me to the authorities?"

"I don't think so. She was an illegal immigrant from Mexico. That was years ago. She's long since been granted permanent residency. She will understand your situation."

"I hope it works out for her and for me. Three days a week of work should give me enough money to get by while still having time for my search."

Kathy left the room to call her neighbor and returned, smiling.

"She believes the two of you can work out the details. She is available this morning if you would like to meet her."

"Wonderful, let me get cleaned up, and I'll go introduce myself. Thank you, Kathy. This is another time you've helped me more than I ever imagined someone would."

Shelly hurried to her room to fix her hair and dress properly before meeting Kathy's friend and her two children. A half-hour later, she was ready.

"Her name is Elena, and she is expecting you. Out the front door, turn right, fourth house, mostly off-white. Two chairs on the front porch, you can't miss it; break a leg!"

Shelly looked at Kathy, a puzzled expression on her face.

"Never mind, I'll explain later. Good luck to you both."

———

A little more than an hour later, Shelly returned and found Kathy reading in the living room.

"Things could not have gone better, Kathy. Thank you so much. Elena and I got on very well together. I met and played with her son, John, and his sister, Sophia. As you said, both are good kids. Elena works at her husband's company and needs someone to be with the kids Mondays, Tuesdays, and Wednesdays. She prefers to pay in cash; no tax record for her or an income record for me. We agreed on a daily amount from 7 AM to 4 PM. I start this coming Monday. Thank you again!"

"I'm very happy for you both."

While Shelly had not been with her long, Kathy enjoyed her company and wanted to help with her search. That required Shelly being able to stay longer than her money would allow. This job, so close to Kathy's house, was perfect for everyone.

Kathy and Shelly spent what was left of the morning talking about how Kathy could help her with her search for Raymond.

"I was thinking about this last night before going to sleep," Kathy said. "If he were from Seattle, there is a chance his family might still be here. If they are, and we can locate them, they could have some news for you. I was also thinking about places he could have frequented, places you could visit. You never know where that might lead you. At the very least, you should enjoy visiting some of them."

Shelly pondered Kathy's suggestion, particularly the part about finding his family.

"We could do that, but I am a little worried about approaching family, particularly his parents, if their son was killed in the war. A stranger from a country they may never have heard of comes asking about their dead son. I don't know."

"You have a point. Why don't we start by visiting some of the sites that many people visit, both tourists and locals? At some point in his life, he would have been to a lot of them. We all did at his age. The Space Needle, Pike Place Market, Pioneer Square, the docks in South Seattle. You'll enjoy it, too."

"Ok, and as always, I see you going out of your way to help me. I appreciate you doing that, Kathy, but I shouldn't take up so much of your time."

"What else would I do? I'm getting as much from you as I hope you are getting from me, even more. You aren't just another house guest. You've brought me a real-life adventure. I should be thanking you. You're not working today, I need to shop for fresh vegetables and fruit, and there are none better in all of Seattle than what we will find at Pike Place Market. OK?"

"Agreed, Kathy, OK."

CHAPTER
FIFTY-FOUR

KATHY PARKED A COUPLE OF BLOCKS FROM THE MARKET, THE TWO OF THEM walking the rest of the way, entering under the large lighted sign telling all that this was Pike Place Market, the large clock next to it showing the correct time. Very little nearby looked like what Shelly expected, including entering through a large opening in the building with no doors.

"You said it was a market where you buy fresh vegetables and fruit. I see that, but I'm surprised everything is so open without doors. This looks similar to outdoor markets in Harare, but it surprises me here in the United States."

"Vegetables, fruit, fresh flowers, and so much more. This is a week-day, crowded, but not nearly as much as it will be on the weekend." Kathy replied, her head turned towards the Athenian bar and restaurant. She paused, turning to Shelly. "Do you know if your friend drank alcohol, maybe liked old bars?"

"I wish I knew that and more, but I don't. We never talked about it. Why do you ask?"

"I thought he might; many soldiers do. The Athenian is over 75 years old, one of the oldest bars in all of Seattle. Let's go for coffee, you'll enjoy seeing it."

They went in, past the larger main bar, back to the smaller one overlooking Puget Sound. Small wooden straight-back booths lined the windows. They decided to enjoy their coffee, standing at the bar, taking in everything and everyone around them.

"Kathy, I can easily imagine him standing here at this bar, having a drink. I almost feel his presence."

"I thought you might, here and elsewhere. Places like this capture some of our being. Someone looking for you in the future might have the same reaction about you as you are having now about your friend. It feels good, doesn't it?"

"It is a good feeling. I first thought I might be sad if I knew or felt he had been here. I am a little, but I also feel a closeness to him. Thank you for bringing me here."

"You're welcome. There are more places to visit today where you might have the same reaction."

Having finished their coffee, they continued walking north through the market, Shelly's head turning left, then right, and back again, attempting and failing to see everything.

"Are you hungry?" Kathy asked.

"I could eat. How about you?"

"Me too, and we are right across the street from another interesting old place, this one a restaurant. Copacabana, founded years ago by Bolivian immigrants. Still family-owned and operated. What do you think, another place Raymond might have been?'

"I don't know, but I want to go in there just as he might have done. It looks like it's on the second floor. How do we enter?"

"This way, the other side of the street, follow me."

Kathy led them to a short staircase leading up to the main entrance. Once seated, Kathy looked at the menu while Shelly's attention was on the restaurant's long, narrow, rectangular interior.

"You'll think I'm making this up, like I feel everywhere you take me will be a place he had been. Maybe so, but I feel Raymond's spirit here as well."

Kathy put her menu down, looking across the table at Shelly.

"I don't think you're making it up. You either have these feelings or you don't. I'm glad you do. The food is good here, and the prices are fair, reason enough for us to have lunch. But the added bonus is that you feel Raymond's presence. Shelly, it is no accident we were in

Athenian's and are now here. I suggested we come to both, but I didn't do so, knowing you would react as you did. No one could have known that. You feel what you do because of your connection to your friend, and his connection to these places and others we can visit."

Shelly sat staring off in the distance, saying nothing. She knew Raymond had been here just as assuredly as she was now. Their lunch arrived, and seeing Shelly's attention was focused elsewhere, Kathy decided it was best to bring the conversation back to their search.

"I think you will enjoy this lunch, Shelly. All fresh, locally grown ingredients prepared following family recipes. And once we're done with lunch, if you like, we can continue exploring."

Hearing her name, smelling the food before them, brought Shelly back from where she had been. Somewhere far away.

"We have wonderful fresh vegetables and fruit in Harare, and the best chefs know how to prepare meals, making them taste even better. Clearly, so do chefs here. Another great suggestion, Kathy."

"Glad you like it. We have time for one more stop. Are you up for it?"

"Absolutely, everything you've shown me to this point has been meaningful. What's next?"

"You've seen it as we drove in and around the city. You can't miss it. However, it's not so much about you seeing it as what it can show you. I first need to get some vegetables and fruit when we're done with lunch."

"You lead, I'll follow."

———

Back in the car, the drive to the Space Needle took less than twenty minutes. Kathy wondered if Shelly thought that might be where they were headed. She must have seen it throughout the day, but hadn't questioned what it was.

"You see that pointy needle-looking tower ahead of us to the left? We're going to the top of it, the observation deck."

"Because you think Raymond would have at some point?"

"Absolutely, almost everyone living in or near Seattle would have once, and a lot more times for many, including me. But that's not why I want to take you there. I'll tell you why once we're on top."

Walking from the car to the Space Needle entrance, Kathy explained some of its history.

"Seattle hosted the World's Fair in 1962. This tower and the surrounding area were a big part of that. Over ten million visitors from all over the world visited the fair during the six months it was open. Shortly after it closed, the Elvis movie came out, and once again, the world was talking about Seattle."

"Elvis movie?"

Kathy looked quizzically at Shelly, expecting to see her smiling, having pretended not to know what she meant. Shelly wasn't smiling.

"Elvis Presley; you've heard of him, haven't you?"

"No, I haven't. What does he do?"

"Well, he is, or was, the biggest star in the world, both as a singer and in movies. He filmed some of "It Happened at the World's Fair" where we are now walking, during the fair. People called him the King of Rock 'n Roll, he..."

Kathy realized none of this registered with Shelly.

"Alright, I see it. You're from Zimbabwe, born a little too late to have heard of him. And, anyway, it's not important that you did. Elvis is not why we're here."

Once off the elevator at the top, Shelly and Kathy walked around the 360-degree observation deck, looking down on the city. When they did, Kathy watched Shelly closely, looking for some response.

"This is beautiful; I see why so many come up here. I wonder what Raymond thought of it his first time."

"That could have been in 1962 or soon after. He would have been a young boy, and like all boys, he would have loved looking down at everything surrounding the tower. You're here now; do you see anything you think might have meant more to him than it does to others?"

Shelly paused, looking left and right and south to the city below them. Her eyes finally settled on shipping docks in the distance, all the cranes, offloading and loading cargo from and destined for faraway ports. Still staring in the distance, she responded.

"He watched those ships, wondering where they came from, where they would go next. I believe Raymond was an adventurer. He would have envied those living and working on those ships."

Shelly shivered as though the air had suddenly turned cold.

"Look around you, Shelly. Do you see all the houses in the distance, south, north, and to the east? Raymond grew up in one of them. He may be there now, or possibly some of his family. Someone who can tell you what happened to him. Are you certain you do not want to search for that house, those people? No guarantees we can find them, but unlike the high school, there are public records we can search for those with the last name Quinn. It's up to you. Think about it, you don't have to decide this minute. Let's head home. We can talk more about it when you're ready."

———

Shelly thought back on this day during the drive home. At first, she wasn't certain visiting Seattle sites would be helpful. Now, she knew it had been, and more importantly, she also knew she would look for public records that might lead her to the house he lived in before going to Vietnam. But still, she had reservations.

I don't want to upset his family. I'm not sure I want to see Raymond if he's married or living with someone. I never really considered that before coming here. It's time I did. Kathy is right; if I want to find out what happened to him, I have to be prepared to accept what I find.

TIRED FROM THE DAY, NOW HOME, KATHY AND SHELLY SHARED A QUICK, easy dinner before heading to their rooms. Shelly showered and lay back on the bed, running through the day's events in her mind, hoping knowing what she should do next would come to her. She was soon fast asleep.

———

Call my brother, he will tell you.

Call who? What was that? Was I dreaming? I have to remember what the dream was about. If that was someone talking to me, who is it, and what do they want?

She lay in bed, her eyes seeing nothing but vague shapes in a room too dark to see clearly. The more she tried to remember, the less she could recall. And then, as if dreaming it again...

Call my brother, he will tell you.

She quickly sat up and turned on the bedside lamp to make sure she was awake, not dreaming. Still not convinced, she got up and went to the bathroom to splash cool water on her face.

Call my brother, he will tell you.

Call your brother? Who is he? How do I find him? Who are you? Raymond?

She looked at the clock on the dresser. Six-thirty AM, the sun was just starting to rise from the east.

Kathy will be up soon, maybe she already is. I want to tell her about this.

Shelly showered again to make sure she was fully awake, leaving no doubt this was not simply a dream. She quickly dressed and left her room. Not finding Kathy in the kitchen, she sat down on the living room couch to wait for her. Less than fifteen minutes later, Kathy walked down the hall, and seeing a light on in the living room, she entered to find Shelly sitting there, her face expressionless.

"Good morning, you couldn't sleep? I sure did."

"Good morning, Kathy. I did sleep and dreamed. I want to tell you about that before breakfast if that's alright with you."

"Certainly, but can it wait while I put on a pot of coffee? Five minutes at most."

"Of course, take your time."

Kathy went into the kitchen, and Shelly waited a moment before getting up to follow her there.

"You will think my dream, if that's what it was, is silly. I do a little, but it was so real."

"Well, the best way to see what I think about your dream is for you to tell me about it. I'll have coffee ready for us in a couple of minutes while you do."

"Yes, again, if it was a dream," Shelly said, somewhat embarrassed, her words dropping away. She questioned herself about what she thought she heard.

"I don't know, Kathy, it was so real. I believe I was sleeping. I heard or dreamed someone talking to me. I woke up trying to make sense of it. But then I heard the voice tell me to 'call my brother, he would tell me'. This time, I was definitely not asleep. I turned on the light next to the bed and saw it was still dark outside. I went to the bathroom and put cool water on my face. The voice again told me to 'call my brother, he would tell me'. I spoke, not dreamed, asking who he was, who his brother was. I asked if he was Raymond. He didn't answer me. By then, it was almost seven. I showered, dressed, and came out here to wait for you."

Kathy could see that Shelly's emotions were at a high point. She poured two cups of coffee, handing one to Shelly.

"Let's have this in the living room, it's more comfortable."

Once seated, Kathy responded.

"We'll talk about your dream or what you heard, but first, I'd like to ask you a couple of questions. Your answers will help me understand what you are struggling to learn. Is that okay with you?"

"Ask whatever you wish."

"This may seem way off from what you want to talk about, but it will all come together when I explain. Have you heard of Carl Jung, and if you have, do you know anything of his writings about what he called Synchronicity?"

Not saying anything, Shelly shook her head.

"Jung was a Swiss psychiatrist, psychotherapist, and psychologist. His theory of Synchronicity is very complex, well beyond my comprehension. I've been thinking that all we saw and did yesterday, and now, what you just told me, may relate to his Synchronicity theory. Let me give you an example. Maybe you were in school, struggling to make sense of something in one of your classes, worried that you would never understand it. And then, without expecting it, someone, possibly your teacher, your parent, a friend, or another student, comes along and explains it to you so you do understand. A mere coincidence? Jung would call that Synchronicity. You had a lot on your mind before we met, even more now, based on what we've done in the few days you've been here. You could have dreamed what you felt you heard while awake. Or it could have been someone, possibly Raymond, attempting to reach you."

Shelly listened carefully to what Kathy said, not entirely grasping the connection between Carl Jung, Synchronicity, and her dream. However, the more she thought about it, the more convinced she became that it was not a dream.

"I didn't dream this, Kathy. I don't know if it has to do with synchronizing or whatever you call it, but I do know it was not a dream. What do I do now?"

"Synchronicity, but you don't have to identify it as being one thing or another. Just focus on what it may mean to you. If you don't know, I have a suggestion."

"What is it?"

"Something or someone is reaching out to you, attempting to help you find what you are looking for. If Raymond has a brother, if the voice is telling you to call him, if we can find him, you should do all you can to make that happen. Do not stop yourself from learning things you need to know. If it is not meant to be, let some other person or thing stop you. If you agree, we can search for Quinns in the phone book, possibly including an address in addition to a phone number. If we find one or more, if you are worried that you will upset a relative, or you cannot handle learning Raymond is dead..."

Seeing Shelly visibly shaken by this last possibility, Kathy paused before continuing.

"...If you are not comfortable contacting them, I can do it for you. If there is a connection, you can then decide what, if anything, you want to do."

Shelly's first reaction was to say she wanted to think it over. But she realized she had said that every time Kathy suggested a new step she might wish to take. She would not do that again.

"I don't need to consider it further, Kathy; that is what we will do. And if we find Quinns to reach out to, I would appreciate you doing that with me."

CHAPTER
FIFTY-SIX

KATHY HAD A PHONE BOOK, BUT SUGGESTED THEY USE THE ONE AT THE local library. More coverage throughout greater Seattle meant more chances of finding Quinns. Breakfast finished, they drove to a nearby library, discovering there were many more local phone books than Kathy had assumed there would be.

"For no better reason than we have to start somewhere, let's begin with those covering neighborhoods with single-family housing in proximity to the Space Needle. Most of that will be north and west of Interstate 5. There are a lot east of the freeway as well, but let's work our way out from the Space Needle so we don't overlook any of them."

Shelly agreed, and they each began looking through books for those named Quinn. Not finding any, Kathy said, "Ok, time to narrow our search, this time centering it around Roosevelt High School. If he went there, he had to live within the school district. Why didn't I think of that before?"

Almost immediately, Shelly found the name Carl Quinn with a phone number, but no address. She paused, uncertain what she wanted to do.

If I tell Kathy what I've found, she will want me or her to call the number. Is that what I want? If not, what has all this been about? Why did I travel halfway around the world if I am not willing to act on what I learn?

A moment of doubt passed.

"Found one, Kathy. Carl Quinn with a phone number, no address."

Kathy took off her reading glasses, sat back in her chair, and, as calmly as possible, responded.

"What do you want to do?"

Shelly wrote down the name and phone number on a piece of paper she brought along for note-taking. She circled and underlined it, quietly tapping the pencil on the phone book, not looking at Kathy. A couple of minutes passed before she replied.

"I will call."

"Are you sure you want to? I told you I would do that for you if you'd rather not."

"I will do it, it has to be me. If I have this number because Raymond wanted me to have it, he would also want me to make the call. You calling, having to say you are calling on behalf of someone else, tells the person on the other end that there are two strangers now involved. No, Kathy, it must be me."

Who would call decided, they put the phone books away, agreeing to come back to continue the search if necessary. But both believed the odds of it being the right person were good. Carl Quinn lives in Raymond Quinn's high school district.

Shelly promised herself she would call.

CHAPTER
FIFTY-SEVEN

SHELLY AND KATHY STOPPED FOR LUNCH ON THE WAY HOME. BOTH WERE hungry, and Kathy thought it a good idea that Shelly call Carl after eating. A quick salad with sourdough bread was perfect. Once home, Kathy decided to check one last time to see if Shelly had any doubts about calling.

"Whatever you think is best. You call, or I can do it for you. I don't want you to be overwhelmed by what may come of it."

"What may come of it? I hadn't thought about that, only that I would tell Carl or whoever answers who I am and why I'm calling. But what *will* I say if he or she tells me Raymond is dead or married?"

"Don't anticipate what will happen. You have good reasons for making the call. Unless some of that has changed, I think it should be you."

"You're right, I'm just stalling. Stay with me, I may need you."

Shelly dialed the number. After a few rings, a man answered.

"Hello"

"Ah, hello, ah, my name is Shelly Bennett. I found your name in the phone book. I see your last name is Quinn. I am looking for Raymond Quinn. Do you know anyone by that name?"

The man hesitated before replying, causing Shelly to become more nervous.

"Who are you, and why are you calling?

"Shelly Bennett. Raymond Quinn was, or is, a friend of mine. We haven't talked in a long time. I am hoping to reconnect with him. We didn't know each other very long or well. All I know is that he said he graduated from Roosevelt High School in Seattle and was in the army in Vietnam. I'm not calling to ask anything from him or you. I only want to hear how he's doing."

"Shelly, I am Carl Quinn, Raymond's brother. It appears you don't know, so this may come as a shock to you. Raymond was killed in Vietnam a little over five years ago. I am sorry, I have to be the one to tell you this."

Kathy saw Shelly's face turn ashen, her eyes focused on nothing, unable to speak or hear what others were saying. She leaned back on the couch, dropping the receiver in her lap.

"Shelly, are you ok? Shelly!" Kathy said as she picked up the receiver.

"Hello, my name is Kathy, a friend of Shelly's. Can you tell me what you said to her? She appears to be in shock."

"I am so sorry. I thought the news might be too much for her, but she did ask. I didn't want to lie to her. I'm Carl Quinn. Raymond Quinn was my brother. He was killed in Vietnam a little over five years ago. Is she ok?"

"She's crying now, a good sign. They wrote to each other while he was still alive. I assume no one in your family knew they were communicating or how to reach her to let her know what happened to him. It's tough finding out after such a long time. It's not your fault, Carl. Assuming she wants to, is it okay if she calls again once she feels better? She has come a long way, halfway around the world, to find out what happened to him. She's not looking for anything other than information. She won't call if you say she shouldn't."

"No, certainly she can call. I don't know that I can tell her much more, but I will share whatever I can."

"Thank you, Carl. I will let her know. And thank you for accepting her call and for your kindness. Goodbye."

Kathy hung up the phone and went to the kitchen for a glass of wine for Shelly. Returning, she saw she was no longer crying, just sitting, watching as Kathy held out the wine for her to take.

"Here, drink this, you'll feel better."

Shelly accepted the glass, but didn't drink, continuing to look at nothing.

"Raymond's dead. He's dead. I've been wondering for five years why he didn't meet me in Singapore, why he stopped writing. *Dead!* That would explain things, wouldn't it?" Shelly said, looking up at Kathy standing before her, not trying to sound funny, just an involuntary, awkward reaction to the news.

"Please take a sip, it will make you feel better."

Shelly did as Kathy requested.

"Assuming you wanted to, I asked Carl if you could call again to learn more. He said he would be happy to talk to you and hoped you would feel better soon. He knew this was a shock for you."

Shelly didn't respond. She just sat holding the glass of wine, looking through, not at Kathy.

"Have another sip, then lie down on the couch. I'll bring you a warm compress for your eyes. You'll feel better after resting a while."

Shelly took a longer sip, setting the glass on the coffee table. Kathy went into the kitchen for the compress and returned, placing it over Shelly's eyes.

"That feels good, Kathy, thank you."

"You're welcome. Hopefully, you will nap. I'll sit with you."

CHAPTER
FIFTY-EIGHT

SHELLY SLEPT FOR HALF AN HOUR, AND WHEN SHE AWOKE, SHE SAW KATHY sitting in a chair across from her, a magazine in her lap.

"How do you feel? You didn't sleep very long."

"Much better. Did you say something about Carl wanting to talk to me, or did I dream that?"

"It wasn't a dream. He said he would be happy to talk to you if you wished. Would you like to do that?"

Raymond is dead. What more do I possibly need to know? I came all this way to learn he is dead.

"You don't have to if you'd rather not, but you may regret it later if you don't. You've come so far. You now know what happened, why Raymond stopped communicating with you. You don't know what more Carl could tell you, and you won't if you don't talk to him again."

"You're right, I should, but not today. I want to think about everything that's happened before calling. I don't know what to ask, but I will in time."

————

Two days passed. Shelly and Kathy did not talk about Raymond or what questions Shelly might ask Carl if she did call.

"There are other places we could visit if you'd like. Places Raymond might have been. Would you like to do that either before or after you talk to Carl? It might help; you never know for certain."

She listened to Kathy's suggestions without participating in the conversation.

"Maybe, but knowing he's dead... I don't know. I'm not here on holiday."

"Please listen to me carefully, Shelly. You are at a crossroads. You can call Carl or decide not to. If you're not going to call, if you don't want to see more of Seattle, how long will you stay here? Don't misunderstand. I'm not asking you to leave. I enjoy having you with me. But this is not your life. You cannot stay indefinitely on a tourist visa; you risk being arrested and deported. It's up to you to decide whether you will call. You said you didn't know what you would ask if you did call. Is that still the case? Maybe Carl has something more he would like you to know. He doesn't know how to reach you. The only way you'll know is to..."

Shelly cut her off in mid-sentence.

"I know that, Kathy. I want to call. I do have some questions. I've just been putting it off. You're right."

Relieved to hear this, Kathy decided to press the issue further.

"Now is as good a time as any. I will stay with you if you like, or leave the room. Here's his number. What do you want me to do?"

Shelly accepted the paper with Carl's phone number, looking at it before answering Kathy.

"Please stay."

She picked up the receiver and dialed the number. After a few rings, she heard Carl's voice.

"Hello."

She momentarily hesitated before answering, prompting Carl to say hello again.

"Carl, this is Shelly. I hope I'm not bothering you. Kathy said you told her it would be okay if I called."

"Absolutely, Shelly. I've been thinking about you, wondering how you are doing."

Shelly was relieved to hear Carl sound so willing to talk with her. Kathy said he would be, but she felt better hearing it from him.

"Thank you, Carl, I appreciate your concern. I was worried about you as well. It's been five years since you went through the trauma of learning about your brother's passing. I imagine by now it is easier for you to accept than it was in the beginning. I hope my calling hasn't forced you back to a place you would rather not be."

"No, Shelly, you haven't. I think about my brother often. I always will. He was older than me, and my parents never told me much about him. Talking to you, who has some connection with him, is good for me. I'm very happy you found me. You've come so far to learn what happened to him. You wouldn't have done that if he weren't important to you. Please ask me anything you like about his passing, when he was growing up, anything at all. I don't know much, but I will tell you what I do know."

Kathy saw Shelly's eyes fill with tears as she listened to Carl. She went to the bathroom and came back with a box of tissues, handing one to her.

"Carl, did your brother ever say anything about me? If not by name, then maybe about someone he was communicating with in letters?"

"I don't remember much about that time. He may have, I don't know. But after your call the other day, I went through some of my parents' things. I found a letter, a partial letter, that Raymond appears to have started and never finished. If you like, I can read it to you, but I'm concerned it will upset you again. You tell me whether or not you want to hear what he wrote."

Shelly again hesitated before answering.

Do I want to hear something I may never be able to forget? Something I may wish I had not heard? I have come too far not to.

Attempting to convince herself as much as Carl that she could handle whatever he read to her, she answered.

"Please do, Carl, Kathy is with me, I'll be ok. If you don't mind, I'll hold the receiver so she can hear as well."

"I'm glad you're not alone."

"Hello, Carl, this is Kathy."

"Hi, Kathy. I told Shelly I found the beginning of a letter from Raymond to my parents. He never finished it. The army sent it along with some of his things. It concerns Shelly. I wasn't sure how she would react when I read it to her. I'm glad you are with her. Shall I read it now?"

Kathy moved to the couch next to Shelly, the box of tissues in her lap. Shelly responded.

"Go ahead, Carl, I'm ready."

July 28, 1970

Dear Mom and Dad,

You remember me telling you about Shelly, the girl from Rhodesia. In mid-August, in two more weeks, I'm taking R&R in Singapore to meet her. One week away from this war with a girl I'm caring more about every day.

"That's all there is."

Hearing this, Shelly immediately began to cry. She tried to stifle herself so as not to make Carl feel this was his fault. But there was nothing she could do. He heard Kathy talking to her, glad she was not alone.

Her arm around her, Kathy said, "It's ok, Shelly, let it out. You needed to hear this, but I know it hurts."

Shelly struggled to regain her composure, her voice cracking.

"Carl, I'm ok; this is not your fault. I'm happy and sad hearing this. Happy to finally have closure regarding Raymond, so sad to learn he is dead. Thank you for sharing it with me."

"You're welcome, Shelly. I know it's difficult for you, but I hope that in time you feel better, and it brings you some relief. There is one more thing I hesitate to mention. Something you may or may not want to know."

Shelly looked at Kathy, her expression asking what she should do. Could she accept hearing anything more emotional than Raymond's last written words to his parents? Words about her. Kathy nodded, silently urging her to tell Carl to continue.

"Please go ahead, Carl."

"In addition to this unfinished letter, I found a small box tied with string, along with a letter from my dad. My parents never accepted that the remains were Raymond's. My dad made it clear that the only person who should open this box was Raymond when he returned home. The box has never been opened, Shelly, but I will open it now if you wish while you are on the phone. Or, if you prefer, you and Kathy are welcome to come to my house, and we will open it together."

Shelly again hesitated before answering, looking at Kathy. As before, Kathy did not respond.

"Carl, if you are certain it would not be a problem for you, I would like to be there when the box is opened."

"I'm glad to hear that, Shelly. I'd also like to meet you in person. Does this afternoon work for you and Kathy?"

Kathy nodded.

"Yes, it does, and I look forward to meeting you as well, Carl."

Kathy wrote down Carl's address. They agreed that Shelly and Kathy would come to his house at 3:30 this afternoon.

CHAPTER
FIFTY-NINE

THOROUGHLY DRAINED FROM THE MORNING'S EVENTS, SHELLY THOUGHT IT would do her good to take a short nap before going to meet Carl. She went to her room to lie down, but soon found sleep impossible. Her mind raced, thinking about all she had learned and would learn this afternoon.

I hoped to find something about Raymond, but I never dreamed it would happen as quickly as it has. Raymond is dead! He's been dead for more than five years. I don't know if I'm better or worse off knowing this. What else will I learn when I meet Carl and we open the box? God, I hope I don't break down crying again; that's not fair to Carl.

Sleep out of the question, Shelly decided to get up and take a short walk before she and Kathy left to meet with Carl. She put on her shoes, left her room, and found Kathy reading in the living room.

"I thought you wanted to nap."

"I did, but my mind has other ideas, trying to grasp all Carl had to say, wondering what else we will learn when we meet with him. I mean, that is what I hoped would happen, but now that it has...I'm overwhelmed. I'm going for a short walk. Maybe that will help me make sense of it all. I won't be long."

"Would you like me to come with you?"

Shelly paused before answering, unsure whether she wanted to be alone or have someone with her.

"No, that's ok, Kathy, I'll be..." She hesitated before continuing. "On second thought, yes, I would like you to come with me. Talking about this rather than thinking about it might help. If you don't mind."

"Not at all. Give me a few minutes to put on some shoes, and we'll head out."

———

The sun was shining, the air temperature just right as they started down the street. It didn't take long for Shelly to start talking about having learned Raymond was dead, that Carl had a box, the contents of which no one will have seen until this afternoon when it is opened with the three of them together.

"He said it's a little box. What could be in it that has me so worked up I can't stop thinking about it? God, please don't let me break down again. Carl went through all of this five years ago, and now this crazy woman from Zimbabwe shows up, forcing him to not only deal with his grief but mine as well."

"Your feelings are natural, don't blame yourself. I'm certain Carl doesn't. You came all this way for answers. You have learned so much. You may learn more this afternoon. Think of yourself as being on a conveyor belt taking you to what you came so far to understand. You put yourself on it, don't get off now. Let it be. Don't try to make sense of it until you know what *it* is."

They walked along in silence, Shelly thinking about what Kathy said.

I'm on a conveyor belt, taking me to what I came to learn. Just let it happen. I've done my part; events are in motion, let it be.

"Kathy, as you so often have since we met, you've helped me put things in perspective. I don't know what will come of our meeting with Carl this afternoon, but I'm glad you will be there with me. I will do my best to accept what happens as it happens."

The rest of their conversation turned to how pleasant the weather was, how glad they both were to be out walking, enjoying the morning. A half-hour later, they were back home, having sandwiches that Kathy prepared for lunch. Soon after, it was time to leave. On their way, still talking about things other than the soon-to-be meeting with Carl, Kathy silently debated whether she should bring the conversation back to the subject at hand, offering Shelly a little more encouragement. Before she could decide what to do, Shelly changed the subject.

"Life's funny, isn't it? We plan, things change, we make new plans, and in the end, we don't know if what is, is better than what might have been. Would I be better off not having come here looking for Raymond? I didn't think so when I began this search. Now I'm not so sure."

"Perfectly understandable, however, there wasn't, and isn't now, just one right answer to your questions and doubts. You know how you felt when you knew nothing. Now, you'll find out how it feels to have learned all there is for you to know. Isn't that the better option?"

Shelly didn't respond; she just continued to look out the windshield as they got closer to Carl's house. She wasn't sure whether knowing or not would be best for her. But Kathy had narrowed the choices down to the most obvious.

Another fifteen minutes later, they arrived at the address Carl had given them. Neither said a word as Kathy turned off the engine, setting the brake. Finally, Shelly spoke.

"I don't think Carl will mind if we are ten minutes or so early, do you?"

"Probably not, but let's give him another five before we go to the door. How are you feeling?"

"Better than I thought I would when we left the house." She turned to face Kathy, smiling.

"Like it or not, I'm on that conveyor belt you mentioned, and there is no getting off now. You have me as ready as I'll ever be for what happens. I'm glad I'm here, very glad you will be with me. Thank you, Kathy."

"You'll do fine, you are a very strong woman. You have endured much these last five years. It may take a while, but that will soon end, starting this afternoon. We're close enough to three, let's go."

———

A few seconds after Kathy knocked, Carl opened the door.

"I hope we're not too early for you. It took less time getting here than I thought it would," Kathy said.

"Not at all," looking at Shelly, he said, "I'm Carl, so happy to meet you both. Please come in."

As they entered, Shelly replied, "Carl, thank you for so much of your time on the phone and now for having us come to your home. I hope this is not a problem for you."

"Not at all, Shelly. In many ways, you finding me is as positive for me as I hope it has been or will be for you. I've had questions regarding my brother's passing, I know you can't answer. But you are the last link to him, which helps me quite a bit. Please, come into the living room. Can I get you something to drink? Iced tea, water?"

"Water would be good for me," Kathy said.

"How about you, Shelly?"

"Water's fine, thank you, Carl."

"Two glasses of water. Have a seat, I'll be right back," he said, leaving the room. Shelly and Kathy sat down on the couch, leaving a chair directly across from them where they expected Carl would sit. Looking around, they saw no family photos, no indication that Carl was living here alone or with someone. That had not come up during their phone calls.

Carl came back into the room carrying two glasses of water. He set them on the table in front of them.

"I don't have much company, so I'm not well prepared for guests."

"I'm the same way, Carl. I rent out a room in my home, that's how Shelly and I met. She's my current boarder. But what I do for them is not the same as what I should do when a friend comes over. I'm not sure I remember what that should be."

Looking at Shelly, Carl replied, "Oh, that's how you know each other. I did wonder how someone from so far away would have a connection to anyone in Seattle."

"It could not have worked out better for me," Shelly said, "I assumed I had booked a bed in a hostel. I ended up with a private room in a beautiful house with a cook, driver, tourist guide, and someone to calm me down when things get overwhelming, all for the price of a hostel."

"And it's worked for me, too, Carl. I'm happy to have been able to help Shelly with her search. But I don't believe she recognizes how much I've enjoyed her staying with me."

"It sounds like it's been good for both of you. Before we get to the box, Shelly, are there any other questions you have that I may be able to answer? It's doubtful I could, but please ask whatever you like."

"I don't think so, Carl. Your situation is similar to mine. We both know very little about what happened to Raymond. Maybe opening the box will tell us something we don't already know. Either way, I am very happy to have found you, and thank you for being so kind to Kathy and me."

Carl stood up as Shelly finished. "I'll be right back with the box; let's start with that and see where it takes us," he said, leaving the room.

Momentarily alone, Kathy and Shelly glanced at each other, saying nothing. Shelly's heart rate increased significantly. Learning that Raymond had been killed in the war was the primary purpose of her trip. Now she would discover the contents of a box that his father so mysteriously said should only be opened by Raymond. Carl returned, a small box with string tied around it in his hands. He set it down on the table in front of Shelly.

"Dad said only Raymond should open this box. He's not here to do that. I think you should do it for him, Shelly."

Shelly stared at the box, her eyes transfixed, wondering what might be in it, questioning whether there was any point in opening it.

Raymond is dead. What more could I possibly need to know?

She looked up to Carl and then to Kathy on her right as though one of them would tell her what to do. Neither of them said anything; both just continued looking at her.

"Carl, I know your father was very explicit in his instructions about opening this box. Only Raymond should do that. Your father believed he would one day return, that he was not dead. We know otherwise. Are you certain you want me to open it? You are a blood relative. I am not, hardly even a meaningful connection to your brother. I think you or possibly some other relative or your wife should open it rather than having me do it."

"There are no others, Shelly, and I'm not married. It's clear from Raymond's words to our parents that you meant much more to him than you realized. I feel that even more after meeting you, knowing you've come so far to find out what happened to him. No, you are the right one, the only one who should open this box."

Looking at it, Shelly imagined Raymond preparing the box to be mailed.

"I understand, Carl," she said, slowly untying the knot of aged string, laying it carefully on the table. She removed the faded multicolored cloth wrapping, placing it next to the string as though both were as important as whatever was in the box. With one last upward glance at Carl, still standing before her, she removed the lid. Inside, she found three military medals: a Bronze Star, a Purple Heart, and an Air Medal. She also found a small envelope, in it one of his dog tags.

She removed the medals, laying them on the table. She pulled the dog tag Raymond had sent her, the one she wore around her neck for the last five years, out from her blouse, comparing it to the one in the box. Looking up at Carl, fighting back tears, her voice breaking, she spoke almost too quietly to be heard.

"They are identical; they both belonged to Raymond."

Carl sat down, neither he nor Kathy saying anything. The gravity of the moment demanded no words be spoken. Shelly leaned back on the couch, her eyes staring, seeing something no one else in the room could see. Her one hand clutching the dog tag that had been in the box all these years, her other hand holding the one she wore around her neck. The two of them separated by thousands of miles, time, and space.

Now, instead of being on the verge of crying, Shelly realized she had no tears left.

CHAPTER
SIXTY

CARL PICKED UP THE MEDALS, LOOKING CLOSELY AT EACH ONE SEPARATELY.

"We received nothing other than what's in this box; three medals and the dog tag," he said, looking at Shelly, still holding it. She realized he hadn't seen it closely.

"I'm sorry, Carl," she said, leaning across the table, her hand outstretched, offering him the dog tag. "This belongs to you. I didn't mean to keep it from you."

He accepted it, looking at it, turning it over in his hand.

"Not me, Shelly. This dog tag and these medals belonged to Raymond, and to you the moment he died," he said, passing the dog tag back to her, laying the unfinished letter on the table next to the box. "Please keep all of it if you like, including the letter he wrote to my parents. I have my memories of him, and now of you."

Once again, silence fell over the room before Kathy quietly turned to Shelly.

"We really should be going; we've taken up much of Carl's afternoon."

"You're right," Shelly said, standing up, facing Carl, still seated across from her. "Carl, I appreciate everything you have done for me, including offering me Raymond's personal effects. There's so little here, are you sure you want me to have any or all of it?"

"I do, Shelly. I would not have offered it to you if I didn't. Please accept it all. That will make me happy, and I know it is what Raymond would want as well. When you get home, will you promise to write me? You represent the only living connection I have to my brother. I would like to hear how you are doing, staying in touch with you."

Shelly moved around the table and hugged Carl.

"Of course I will. I have no brothers, is it okay if I think of you that way?"

"Certainly, why didn't I think of that, sister?" he said, smiling, turning toward Kathy. "And it was a pleasure meeting you, too, Kathy. We're both local, how about having lunch or dinner with me sometime?"

"I'd like that, Carl, thank you, and I'll take my hug now as well." She said.

Shelly put the medals and dog tag back in the box, picking up the letter, the outer cloth wrapping, and the string along with it. Seeing this, Carl said, "I can throw away any of that you don't want to keep, Shelly."

"No, thank you, Carl, I will keep it all. It was together all these years for me to receive today. I can't part with any of it now."

Shelly and Kathy walked to the front door, thanking Carl, saying goodbye, and promising once more to stay in touch. Before starting back to Kathy's house, Shelly reflected on the day's events.

"I don't know if this is right, but I feel very good about how things have turned out, like a weight has been lifted off me. Carl was all I could have hoped he'd be, and I will write him."

"I'm glad you recognize that, Shelly. It would have been easy for you to miss in your grief. I can see you are sincerely thankful. You came such a long way, hoping to find what you wanted and needed to know. Short of having found Raymond alive, you couldn't have imagined a better outcome. So, instead of going straight home, I have another place in mind for dinner tonight. We won't ever forget today, but let's try to briefly put the emotion aside and enjoy a reasonably fun girls' night out. What do you say?"

"Absolutely, we deserve it."

———

Their dinner, drinks, the restaurant atmosphere, and most of all the company, combined to make a wonderful evening for both of them. For the first time since arriving at Kathy's home after almost two days of traveling across the globe, Shelly was at peace. She did not know what the future held for her, but tonight, whatever that would be, was of no concern.

CHAPTER
SIXTY-ONE

WHAT WILL YOU DO?

Is there something more for me to do?

Have you learned all you want and need to know?

Raymond is dead, and I can't stay here indefinitely. What else is there?

You committed suicide. You have an immortal existence yet to be determined. I am here to help you find what that is. You and Raymond share something in common. You are both dead. Have you ever wondered about his immortality?

I haven't, but I would like to know. Could we exist together in some way?

Not if one or both of you decide there is no point in looking for the other.

I will continue to look for Raymond, but I don't know where or how to do that.

You will know when it is time to leave a place, person, or situation. You must first leave a place to go to a new place. When you arrive there, be open to new people who might lead you to new situations. No one can help you do this; only you can know where you should go, who you should meet.

CHAPTER
SIXTY-TWO

THE NEXT MORNING, AFTER BREAKFAST, KATHY AND SHELLY SAT IN THE backyard enjoying a second cup of coffee. Very relaxed after a good night's sleep, their conversation was more about Kathy's life than Shelly's search for Raymond. Until, as she always did, Kathy brought the conversation back to Shelly and her plans.

"Have you given any thought to what you'll do next?"

"Yes and no. I know I need to leave at some point, but I have this feeling there is something more I need to do here. I have time left on my visa. My money situation is adequate. Of course," Shelly smiled at Kathy before continuing, "You might be ready for me to go."

"You know that's not so. You've been the best, most accommodating, appreciative boarder I've ever had. And talk about interesting," Kathy smiled at Shelly, "No one comes even close to you. No, I'm in no hurry to see you go. You say you have a feeling there's something more you need to do here. Any ideas what that is?"

"Nothing specific, but I do want to go back to Pike Place Market to look around some more. So much of what I saw there made me feel as though Raymond saw it all, too. I want to see if I still feel that way."

"Not a problem, we can go back there..." Shelly interrupted her.

"Kathy, please don't be offended. I need to go by myself. Whatever this vague notion of me going there is about, I need to do so alone. But

I want us to go there again before I leave. I enjoyed our first time, I'm sure I will again. Just not this time. I hope you understand."

"No offense taken, of course, I understand. You're not a normal tourist, and nothing about your stay here has been normal. By all means, go where your heart tells you to go. I can drive you there if you like. If not, it's a simple half-hour bus ride with no changes. You can't miss the stop for the market, two blocks east on Pike at 3rd. Note the bus number; that will be your ride back to where you got on."

"Thanks, Kathy. I'm very comfortable riding buses. I do so much of the time at home. Seattle buses are much cleaner and safer than those in Harare. I'll be fine."

"When do you plan to go?"

Shelly looked at her watch.

"Nine o'clock, plenty of time left today. If it's alright with you, I think I'll get ready and go now. That would give me time to look around and still be back for dinner with you here or at a restaurant, whichever you prefer."

"Let's eat in tonight, I have a recipe for a minimum of two I've been wanting to try again. I think you'll like it. Get ready, have fun. I'll be here when you return."

An hour later, Shelly walked to the bus stop just in time for her bus to arrive less than a minute later. Once on board, she settled by a window to see what most other riders ignored.

I understand why. When you ride the same bus, taking the same route every day, there's nothing you haven't seen.

But it was all new to Shelly, and she paid close attention, wondering how much of this Raymond might have seen.

How often did he ride the bus, any bus? Where did he go? What did he do before going into the army, going to Vietnam? I'll never know.

Traffic was light, and in less time than Kathy said it would be, the bus was downtown heading north on 3rd. Shelly watched the street signs, assuming she would not know when to pull the cord signaling the driver she wanted to get off in time for him to stop. If not, when she saw they were passing Pike, she would pull it and get off one short block later. But the closer they got to downtown, she realized even that would not be necessary. Other riders were pulling the cord most every stop; she wouldn't have to. A few blocks later, approaching Pike, she heard the signal for the driver. The bus pulled to the curb, and she got off at Pike and 3rd as Kathy had instructed. She looked to see that her bus back to where she boarded would be number 7.

So far, so good, where to now?

Looking west on Pike, Shelly saw the Pike Place Market sign above the entrance. That would be her starting point. Still unsure where to go, she stopped on the northeast corner of Pike and 1st, taking in all the people and energy spilling out of the market.

I've been to Athenian's and down the street for lunch with Kathy at Copacabana. I've had my coffee. I'll walk through the market, starting from the north end.

Shelly crossed the street, walking north outside the market, entering at the opposite end, immediately questioning her decision to come.

What did I expect would happen? I'd walk along, and some revelation regarding Raymond would come to me? There has to be more to it than just that, much more.

She reached into her jacket pocket, feeling the box containing Raymond's dog tag, his medals, and the last letter to his parents in her room at Kathy's. Just touching it made her feel closer to him. She concentrated on the goods vendors were selling, much of it made outside the US in Mexico or Asia. But she also found leather goods, paintings, olive oil, jams, seasonings, vegetables, fruit, and flowers created, grown, or crafted locally. Her outlook softened.

Raymond wouldn't be walking along whining about having come here; I shouldn't either. Chances are, I will never be back here again. I will enjoy being here now.

Shelly was now hungry. With so many choices of places to eat, the only decision she had to make was what to eat and where to eat it. She recalled walking by a shop that sold sausages, either to go or cooked and served in their small dining area.

Where was that? It smelled so good when Kathy and I passed it, very near the Athenians. That's what I want.

She continued walking through the market, and past Athenians on the same side of the walkway, she came to Uli's. People were ordering sausages to go, while others were served sausage sandwiches with fries and beer inside. She went in and sat at the last available table with room for only one more person. She took the box out of her jacket pocket, briefly looking at it before placing it on the table near her.

"What can I get you?" the waiter asked as he handed Shelly a menu. "We have two beers on tap, one local, one German, some bottled beer you see in the cooler, canned soft drinks as well, and water you pour yourself to your left."

"I'll have the German draft and will give you my sandwich order when you bring the beer."

The waiter left Shelly looking at the sausage choices, all of which sounded very good to her. When he returned and set her beer down, she was ready to order.

"I'll have a Thuringer on a hard roll, nothing on it, with fries."

"You got it. Be patient, there are a few ahead of you."

Shelly smiled, hoping to demonstrate she had no intention of not being patient and polite.

Moments later, an Asian man walked in. He looked around, and seeing only the empty seat at Shelly's table, he approached her.

"Excuse me, I don't mean to bother you, but this is the only seat left. Would it be okay with you if we shared the table?"

Shelly's initial reaction was to say she'd rather eat alone. But something made her change her mind.

'You must first leave a place to go to a new place. When you arrive, be open to new people who might lead you to new situations.'

This is a new place, this is a new person. Why not?

"Certainly, please sit down." Looking at the other tables, she continued. "The plates are small; we can make it work."

"I'm Don. Thank you for sharing your table. I was walking by, and everything smelled so good. I was instantly hungry. And now that I see your beer, I'm thirsty too."

Shelly smiled, hoping the sip of beer she'd just had did not leave her with a foam mustache.

"I'm Shelly, and this beer is good. The waiter will tell you your drink options are this German draft I'm having, a local draft, other bottled options, and soft drinks in the cooler. Self-serve water to your right. Maybe I should be waiting tables instead of eating here."

Don laughed, "Maybe you should; you did that very well. Based on your accent, I assume you're not a local. You have that slightly over-whelmed look many tourists have when they first encounter Pike Place Market. You're not British or Australian. My guess is you're from somewhere in Africa, most likely South Africa, the southern part of the continent, not the country itself. Correct?"

Shelly laughed, "Yes, you are, you got so much of it right, any guesses what my address is?"

Don smiled before responding. "No. I'm good, but not that good, but let me see if I can guess the country. You sound as though you completed university. Being honest, how happy are you with your country's government?"

The question surprised Shelly. She decided to answer honestly without going into detail.

"Let's just say I am disappointed in my country's government."

"Fair enough, that leaves a few possibilities to be considered, but I will guess, Zimbabwe."

A genuine look of surprise on her face, Shelly responded. "How you got to that in the little time we've been talking is a major surprise. But yes, you are right, I am from Zimbabwe."

Don laughed again, his face similar to how a child looks when they correctly guess something their parents did not expect them to know. Holding out his hand, he continued.

"Like you, I'm a tourist, one difference being, I've probably been here a few weeks longer than you."

Shelly shook his hand. "Nice to meet you, Don. Where are you from?"

"Originally, Vietnam, but I'm here now attempting to turn my tourist visa into something more permanent."

The waiter approached, taking Don's drink and sandwich order, telling him to be patient as he had Shelly.

"What brings you to Seattle, Shelly?"

"I'm here as a tourist, but I also have some personal business to take care of. That's almost done. I'll be leaving soon. How about you?

"Similar. What have you seen so far beyond the market?"

"Let's see, in the market, Athenians, here, across the street, Casablanca, further away, the Space Needle, and a few restaurants by the lake. That's about it; most of my time has been spent on the personal stuff."

The waiter approached with Shelly's sandwich and Don's beer.

Looking at Don, he said, "We're getting caught up; your sandwich is coming shortly."

"Thank you," Don said, picking up his beer, taking a sip as the waiter turned to go back to the kitchen.

Shelly cut her sandwich in half and took a bite.

"I can see from the expression on your face you're pleased."

"Beyond pleased. I've had brats before, but never a Thuringer. Don't know why I decided to try it, but I'm very happy I did. You ordered that as well, didn't you? You won't be sorry."

"I don't believe I've had it before, but seeing you enjoying yours, I'm looking forward to it."

A few minutes later, the waiter returned with Don's order.

"Thuringer on a hard roll, Dijon on the side. Enjoy," he said, quickly turning to head back to the kitchen.

"Ok, time to try," Don said before taking a bite. "Oh, you are right, this is good. Thuringer. I'll have to remember that."

Their conversation regarding the food and their beers continued throughout lunch until Don brought it back to Shelly.

"There is a lot to see and do in and around Seattle, more than most tourists have time to enjoy. And, of course, where else would people who like coffee find such a selection? Are you a coffee drinker? No, wait, given your British upbringing, you more likely prefer tea, correct?"

Shelly wiped her lips with a napkin.

"Both depending on the circumstance, although I have had more coffee, less hot tea, the last couple of weeks." Briefly looking around, she continued. "Probably no coffee or tea here, but either sounds good."

"We're across the street from one of Seattle's premier Starbucks at 1st and Pike, a Seattle institution. When we finish here, if you have time, let's head over there and have coffee or hot tea on me. What do you say?"

Shelly started to decline, but quickly decided otherwise.

"Why not? Sure, I'm open to new places," she said, placing the box back in her jacket pocket.

Lunch over, they paid their checks, and Don led the way out of the market, across 1st to the Starbucks on the northeast corner.

"You may wonder why this Starbucks is different from all the others. Before we go in, turn around facing the market. See that large Public Market Center sign on the roof? Sooner or later, and it's usually sooner, almost every Seattle tourist will find their way to this intersection, and that sign welcoming them to the famous Pike Place Market. And directly across the street, where we're now standing, is this Starbucks. Many mistakenly believe it to be the original. They later go home, telling friends they were in the first Starbucks, never knowing it's not. That one is across the street from the market, about a block north. You can't miss it because, rain or shine, there's almost always a line of people waiting to go inside. Those folks *can* go home and brag to their friends."

As he had when they were having lunch, Don finished with a big smile as though he had shared something Shelly would not have otherwise known. He appeared so pleased with himself, she didn't have the heart to tell him Kathy had pointed all that out to her on their visit to the market. Instead, she responded with just one word, hoping to sound convincing.

"Interesting."

Don held the door open for her, and the two of them went inside.

CHAPTER
SIXTY-FOUR

SHELLY'S LEFT HAND WAS IN HER JACKET POCKET HOLDING ON TO THE BOX, a folded newspaper under her right arm, as they approached the barista waiting to take their order. A large coffee for Don, hot tea for Shelly. Moments later, their drinks in hand, they looked for seats, and seeing two opposite a man sitting by himself, they started toward them. Shelly spoke to him as they approached.

"Excuse me, are these seats taken?"

"No, all yours."

She smiled and thanked him as she and Don sat down, resuming their conversation, Shelly answering a question Don asked at the counter. The man sitting across from her, hoping to look as though he was not paying attention, was intrigued by her accent.

"How long, I can't say. Long enough to take care of my business before my visa expires. Soon, I suppose."

"Then what?" Don asked.

"Good question. I can't or don't want to go back to Salisbury, not with the booger of government there now. You can't expect people with little or no education and no experience governing to do well immediately. I hope they do, honestly. God knows they can't do worse than those they have replaced. But not for me. No, thank you! I was born there; I won't die there. Let someone else sort the mess."

Shelly's attitude since coming into Starbucks had changed. Before, she sounded happy, at the very least not irritated as she now appeared to be.

The man across from them looked out the window, still doing all he could to hear every word the woman and Asian man sitting across from him said. He knew nothing about either of them, but the woman fascinated him. Very attractive, her accent familiar but different, and clearly in charge of the conversation with her companion. He hoped to learn more about her before she left.

Starbucks had become more crowded, with many people standing and no seats available. He worried others would wonder why he continued sitting long after finishing his coffee. But he would not give up his seat as long as the woman across from him remained in hers. He noticed the Asian man spoke with a slight accent, which he guessed was Vietnamese.

"So crowded here, maybe we should finish our drinks and go elsewhere. Possibly the place the barista suggested. It doesn't sound far—a short cab ride, I think."

Don turned toward the man sitting across from him, still looking out the window.

"Excuse me, are you from around here?"

"Yes. I live in the building across the street."

"About how far south is it to the docks? Specifically, the corner of S Massachusetts and Alaskan Highway?"

"Not far. Depending on how much you like to walk, and the shoes you're wearing, it's walkable."

"Walking's great, but it's too cold today. We'll take a cab if we go."

"Head south, any cab driver will know the way. Are you looking for anything specific? Maybe I can help you."

"Yes, actually, the barista recommended a place called Other Worlds Coffee. Much less crowded, more local people, and interesting ones at that. Just what we're hoping to find."

Shelly stared at the man as he and Don discussed the distance and how to get to Other Worlds.

"I often look for alternatives to this place myself. Are the two of you here on vacation, maybe business?" The man said.

Still looking directly at him, Shelly replied.

"I'm not, I have personal matters to attend to. You say you live here. Do you mind my asking what you do?"

Shelly's question struck him as a little strange coming from someone he didn't know. He wanted to sound as casual in his answer as she was direct. He began with a small laugh, smiling.

"Good question, one I often ask myself. I did work near here until the company I worked for was sold. The exit package was good enough to make me a man of leisure for a long time. Maybe too long with too much leisure. I'm generally more bored than not."

Aware he had offered more information than she asked for, he paused before continuing.

"What about you?"

"I'm sorry, my name is Shelly, and this is..." She stopped and turned to Don. "I am so embarrassed, and bad with names, what did you say your name was?"

Don smiled, looking at Ray as he extended his hand.

"Not a problem, I'm Don. Good to meet you, a local at that!"

"Good to meet you, Don. You, too, Shelly. I'm Ray. I initially thought you both might be tourists."

Still smiling, looking around at those around them, Don replied. "No, but I see many others here who probably are. It's understandable that you might guess we were, too."

"Yes, with cruise ships a block away, this Starbucks gets a lot of them. If you don't mind me asking, Don, are you, by chance, Vietnamese? You have a slight accent; that would be my guess. None of my business, just curious."

"Yes, very good, and you might also have guessed my legal name is not Don. I only go by that because Americans have no hope of dealing with my Vietnamese name, Đoàn ăn Giáp. Đoàn is my family name. I considered using Van as a first name, but ultimately decided to become Don Van."

A big smile on his face, looking back and forth between Ray and Shelly, he continued.

"Only in America can we become anything we wish to be, including a completely different person, name and all."

"True," Ray said, looking back at Shelly.

"You have an accent as well, one I can't place."

"I'm from Rhodesia, renamed Zimbabwe by the people now in charge."

The abrupt way she answered and the neutral look on her face suggested to Ray that this was not a subject she wished to discuss further. A few uncomfortable moments of silence passed before she turned to Don.

"We've had our coffee and tea, and I'd rather not go to Other Worlds today. But I am interested. How about meeting there tomorrow morning?"

Not waiting for Don to answer, she turned to Ray.

"And since you are a bored 'man of leisure,' please join us, Ray."

Once again, her directness surprised him.

"Thank you, Shelly, much appreciated." Looking at Shelly and Don, he continued, "But I don't want to intrude on your time in Seattle."

"Nonsense," Don said, "and we're not together. We just met in Pike Place Market and decided to have coffee and tea. Please join us! Based on what the barista said, it is a must-stop for people willing to go however far necessary to find something new and interesting. And from what you said, it's not that far, regardless."

Ray was intrigued, mostly by Shelly but increasingly by Don as well. And truth be told, he had nothing to do tomorrow as he didn't most any day.

Standing up, ready to leave, Shelly spoke.

"You must, Ray, I insist! Other Worlds Coffee, S Massachusetts and Alaskan Highway, tomorrow morning. Shall we say around 10?"

Ray stood to shake both their hands.

"Well, I'm out of excuses. Why not? Sure, I'll be there!"

"Great!" Don replied. "You said you're bored, so try something new. I'm looking forward to seeing you tomorrow."

Don and Shelly walked out the door, stopping outside. After a minute or so of conversation, they shook hands. Don turned north, heading up 1st Street, Shelly started east on Pike, a direction that would take her past Ray, sitting by the window.

Not wanting her to think he'd been watching, he picked up the newspaper she left behind on her chair, hoping to appear as though he was reading.

Once outside the window from Ray, Shelly tapped on the glass to get his attention. He looked up, feigning surprise, followed by a smile. Shelly pointed to the number 10 on her watch, mouthing, 'See you tomorrow morning, 10, Other Worlds.'

Ray nodded; he would be there.

For the first time in a long time, he felt happy with what happened. While knowing little about Shelly or Don, he looked forward to tomorrow.

———

Momentarily lost in his thoughts, Ray missed the first time the woman spoke, now hearing her the second time.

"Excuse me, is your friend coming back? I wondered if this chair is open."

Ray looked up to the woman standing to his side, gesturing at the seat Shelly had been sitting in moments before.

"Oh, I'm sorry. No, she's gone, make yourself comfortable," Ray said, looking at the chair, seeing a small box he assumed belonged to Shelly. It was now on the chair cushion by the chair arm.

"She left it, and when I grabbed the paper, I must have knocked it onto the seat cushion."

Ray reached over to pick up the box. "This belongs to my friend. I'll see that she gets it."

The woman thanked him and sat down, looking out the window, blowing on her steaming cup of coffee.

There was no doubt in Ray's mind that he would meet Shelly tomorrow at 10, and he now had an ironclad reason to do so: to return the little box. He looked at it, turning it slowly around in his hand.

Realizing she could have missed it and her newspaper, and might be back for both, he did not want her to catch him studying the box. He looked over his shoulder in the direction she had walked—no sign of her.

He lightly shook the box, hoping the woman sitting across from him wouldn't notice. It did not appear to be sealed. He could open it if he chose, precisely what he desperately wanted to do. He told himself he was not prying into her business. Just hoping to find something that would help him return her private property. But he knew this was unnecessary justification since he could return it to her tomorrow at Other Worlds.

He waited another ten minutes, occasionally looking out the window to see if Shelly might be hurrying back. When she didn't appear, he finally summoned the courage to open the box.

Carefully removing the lid, he looked inside at a white envelope, yellowed with age, folded in half. He looked over his shoulder once more before taking the envelope out of the box, placing it in his lap. It was not sealed, he opened it and found a thin piece of tissue paper covering a single dog tag. His heart raced as he picked it up, half expecting Shelly to appear, demanding an explanation of what he was doing with her property.

He read the words stamped in steel:

CHAPTER
SIXTY-FIVE

What a night! It took me forever to get to sleep, and no sooner had I and it was time to get up. But for what? Another trip to Starbucks for coffee, I'll probably drink here in the apartment. What's the point?

It was then that Raymond remembered meeting Shelly and Don at Starbucks across the street from his building the day before.

I agreed to join them today at what did they call it? Other Worlds Coffee? That can't be, I dreamed them, our conversation, even Shelly's and Don's accents. A woman from Zimbabwe, a man from Vietnam. Shelly forgetting her little white box...definitely a dream.

This last thought stopped Ray cold.

If I have that box, it could not have been a dream!

Still in bed, Ray threw back the covers, got up, and rushed to the living room, looking for the little white box. Not finding it, he looked in the kitchen and bathroom. Again, nothing, he walked back into the bedroom to get ready for... *just another day with no purpose. I dreamed it all.*

Showered and dressed, having had the same simple breakfast he had every day, Ray looked out the window to the street below, to Starbucks on the corner.

Why not? I have nothing else to do—no point changing my pointless routine.

Ray put his wallet in his pants pocket, his watch and jacket on, before picking up his keys and putting them in the jacket pocket. His hand touched something unexpected.

The box! I have the box, it was not a dream! Don and Shelly are real. They expect me to meet them today at Other Worlds Coffee. Oh God, the address! Somewhere south by the docks. She gave me the address; why didn't I write it down? What do I do? I can't just go down to the docks, wandering around looking for it. What time is it? What time did they say to meet them there? Ten o'clock, I remember the time, but where? Wait, Don said the Starbucks barista recommended the place and gave them the address. If he's working today, I can ask him; he'll know.

Now with purpose, Ray quickly got on the elevator, down to the lobby, and out the front door, hoping the Starbucks barista from yesterday would be there working.

"He'll tell me the address, it's only 9:30, I have time. I can make it by 10.

He hurriedly crossed the street and went into Starbucks, seeing two people in line before him. He also saw the barista from the previous day looking at him.

He remembers me and probably his conversation with Don and Shelly.

The two ahead of him finished their order and moved away from the counter. Ray approached the barista.

"Good morning, what can I get you?

Ray struggled to calm himself, not to appear overly anxious.

"Well, nothing to drink or eat, but you can help me. Do you remember the tall Asian man and woman you served yesterday afternoon? You recommended a coffee shop down by the docks. They sat across from me, telling me about it, asking me to meet them there this morning at 10. I agreed, but I don't recall the address. Can you tell me where it is? I'll write it down," Ray said, pulling out a pen prepared to write down what the barista told him.

"I do. It is a quiet place, certainly more so than here, no offense to my employer," he said, winking at Ray. "Other Worlds Coffee at S Massachusetts and Alaskan Highway. Take a cab, you'll make it. When you arrive, look carefully; you could miss it. Many people I've recommended it to have. Don't be one of them."

Ray thanked him, leaving $2 for his time and information. He rushed out the door and was soon in a cab heading south on 2nd.

CHAPTER
SIXTY-SIX

THE TAXI PULLED UP TO THE CORNER OF S MASSACHUSETTS AND ALASKAN Highway as Ray requested. Not seeing anything that looked like a coffee shop, he hesitated, getting out.

"Are you sure this is it? I'm looking for Other Worlds Coffee, supposedly at this intersection."

"Never heard of it, but this is where you said you wanted to go. $10.75, please, tip not included."

Ray gave the driver $12 and got out of the cab. He could see in all directions. Nothing looked like a coffee shop had ever been near here. He crossed to the beginning of Colorado, and a chain-link fence keeping pedestrians and traffic from passing under the viaduct. Seeing nothing, he turned back east, looking to where he had crossed the street moments before, now wondering whether to walk back or look for a cab. One required time, the other money. Ray had both.

But he did miss one thing. Looking down, an exceptionally large gray cat was sitting a few feet to his left.

How did I miss you? A cat, fat from hunting rats on the waterfront, no doubt.

The cat stared at Ray, not blinking, his expression never changing.

"Not the nicest part of town, is it, Ray?"

The voice coming from behind caused Ray to turn, expecting to see the fence blocking his way. The fence was there, now with a gate, and behind it, he saw Don walking toward him. Confused how Don was able to find this place while he couldn't, he replied.

"I suppose not, but...did you have any trouble finding this place? I sure did. Where is it? I still don't see a coffee shop."

Fewer than twenty feet from the gate, Don turned and smiled, pointing to the entrance to Other Worlds.

"We're here, and the coffee's on me."

Ray looked where he pointed, and, to his disbelief, there was a small building with an Other Worlds Coffee sign above the door.

How did I not see any of this? No gate, pathway, cat, or coffee shop!

"Confusing, I know," Don said, as though hearing Ray's thoughts. "But now that you're here, you'll never forget it. Come on in, it's warm inside."

Ray turned toward him, and although still confused and a little concerned, he did as Don said.

Once through the door, he found this coffee shop unlike any he'd been in previously. As the Starbucks barista said, much quieter, no obvious tourists or homeless. No more than a half dozen customers in a space that could easily hold three times as many. A room much larger inside than it appeared from the outside.

The furniture included a half dozen overstuffed leather chairs positioned throughout in groups of two, with as many tables for two to four near them. Music was playing—an instrumental version of a war protest song Ray liked because it took him back to Seattle forty-seven years earlier, when he was a young soldier before shipping out to Vietnam.

His initial reluctance to follow Don lessened, possibly because there were other customers and the room was warm. Or was it something else? Ray often questioned things and the motives of people he didn't know, as though they threatened him. As comfortable as everything seemed, he looked for something unsettling, soon finding it.

Quickly scanning the room, he saw many differences from all other coffee shops, starting with the windows. There weren't any. The artificial lighting was also different. No visible lighting fixtures, yet the room was well-lit in a warm, comfortable way, like sunlight filtered through trees on a sunny mid-spring day in the northwest forest not far from where he now stood.

This last thought jarred him back to reality.

Still looking toward the door, his back to the coffee bar, Ray heard a familiar voice.

"What would you like, Ray?"

He turned toward the counter, expecting to find someone he recognized. Don and a barista stared back at him.

"What can I get you, Ray?"

"Grande bold," Ray replied.

"I told the barista you might have missed this place had I not come along."

"No doubt about it," Ray said, staring intently at the barista. "I'd all but given up and began wondering how best to go home."

Ray thought he might know the barista from somewhere other than this place he had never been to before today. No one from his work life. No apparent connection with his few acquaintances, but familiar, nevertheless. He felt uncomfortable, deciding this was his normal fear of new things and people. The barista put two coffees on the bar, and seeing this, Ray reached for his wallet.

"No need, Ray. I've taken care of it," Don said, walking toward two leather chairs, their coffees in hand. "Glad you made it! Have a seat."

Ray sat down in one of the chairs next to Don, while Don sat in the other. Bewildered, looking about, it suddenly occurred to Ray that he hadn't seen Shelly. He looked at his watch, 10:15.

"Shelly didn't come with you? It's after 10. Did she let you know she'd be late?"

Don looked at his coffee, blowing on it, stirring the hot liquid with steam rising from the cup.

"She was here. She couldn't stay and only came to say goodbye. She told me to tell you that, assuming you came."

"She's been here and gone, didn't want to leave without saying goodbye," Ray said, as though paraphrasing Don's words would enable him to make sense of what was happening. It didn't.

"You look confused, Ray. That's understandable. Shelly is, too. She wished she could have stayed to meet you here today, but that wasn't possible. She said it was time for her to move on to different places, people, and situations. She said you would understand. She also said you have something that belonged to her. Something she wanted you to have. She didn't tell me what it was, only that you would soon understand if you didn't already."

Ray stood up from the chair, looking around the room. The others there when he first entered now gone; the chairs they sat in empty—no cups or saucers on the tables. The room's contents were disturbing in some way he couldn't explain. His back to Don, Ray asked a question, hoping to sound as though he was not interested in the answer.

"Have you been here before?

Don didn't answer.

"Does any of this strike you as strange? Is this what you expected when the Starbucks barista recommended that you and Shelly come to this place?"

"To a point, maybe, but everything changed when Shelly decided she could not be here today with you. She had to move on. I do too, and so do you, Ray. But there is one more issue. Shelly said you have something that belonged to her. Something she wants you to have. Do you know what she was referring to?'

The question surprised Ray as though it were something he should have remembered without prompting from Don. He turned to face him, his hands checking his pants pockets, followed by those in his jacket. Feeling nothing, he responded nervously, stuttering.

"I...I don't. I thought I did, but that was just a dream."

Don stood up and walked toward the wall with travel posters. Looking up at them, his back to Ray, he spoke.

"You don't know what Shelly was talking about or what she said belonged to her that she wanted you to have. You don't know, but you can find what that is and more, Ray. It's time for you to leave this place, these people, this situation."

CHAPTER
SIXTY-SEVEN

"LADIES AND GENTLEMEN, THIS IS YOUR CAPTAIN SPEAKING. WE WILL BE starting our descent into V.C. Bird Airport shortly and should be on the ground in 40 minutes. The temperature is a comfortable eighty-one degrees Fahrenheit, twenty-seven degrees Celsius. It's been a pleasure having you fly with us today. I hope you've enjoyed the trip. Flight attendants, please prepare the cabin for landing."

Shelly looked out the window, hoping to see things as she remembered them so many years ago. She considered staying where she had that first trip, but decided against it. Instead, she chose the Antigua Inn hostel where Raymond had stayed.

I hope I'm doing the right thing. I'm not even sure why I decided to come here. What do I expect to find? How different might things have turned out had I gone with him to Germany? Why didn't I? It wasn't because he said he was going to East Berlin. I knew that was just talk. How different would my life now be?

The airport had been enlarged since Shelly's first and only visit, including long-overdue improvements to baggage claim that allowed her to clear immigration and customs far more quickly. Once outside, she made her way to the shuttle that would take her to Five Islands Village and the short walk to Antigua Inn.

Shelly looked intently at the driver as he placed her luggage in the back of the shuttle. She knew she wouldn't recognize him; it had been too many years and likely numerous drivers since she was last here. After waiting for three additional passengers, the shuttle started its short trip to Five Islands.

"Everybody happy to be here in beautiful Antigua?" The driver called out as he drove past houses, which, to Shelly, looked as if they hadn't changed at all since her first trip. Hearing only one or two muffled responses, he tried again.

"Come on, people, this is your holiday. Be happy! Are you happy? You make me sad if you're not happy."

This time, Shelly and the other three passengers answered enthusiastically; they were happy to be there. Shelly wasn't sure she was, not as much as the driver wanted all of them to be. But she would act as though she were.

Based on what she could hear, the couple was returning to celebrate their fifth anniversary. She didn't know why the young woman sitting alone directly in front of her was there.

About my age, my first time here. Oh, the advice I could give her. But she would no more want to hear it from me than I would have from some older woman I didn't know when I was her age.

The shuttle pulled to a stop in Five Islands Village. Shelly got out, collected her luggage, and looked around for familiar places and things.

Not all that different. The chemist store, the same shops catering to tourists looking for souvenirs, a very small grocery store. Maybe a couple of new restaurants.

And then she saw it. Caribbean Paisano. Memories of dinner there with Raymond washed over her. She hadn't thought of it in years, but now it was as though that restaurant and Shelly had been here all along.

She smiled. *What was that beer? It was so good, and we had too many of them. Wally? Something like that? How could I forget?*

She approached the driver, now waiting in the shuttle for passengers returning to the airport.

"I was here years ago. There was a beer I enjoyed. The name started with a W. Maybe Wally or something similar?"

"Wadadli, what the island used to be called. Good beer, not too strong unless you drink too many," the driver said, winking at her. "Maybe that's why you no remember the name?"

Shelly laughed. "That's it, and as for drinking too many of them is concerned, I'll never tell. I'm staying at Antigua Inn, can you point me to where that is?"

"Sure, no problem, one block behind us, turn left, you can't miss it," he said, looking at her two suitcases. "I'd drive you there, but I have to wait for people going to the airport."

"That's not necessary, I can walk, thank you," Shelly said, handing the driver another dollar for the information.

———

Once at the hostel and settled in a room she would share with two other women, she lay on the bed to plan her first evening in St. John's. But her mind and body soon had another idea, and she was fast asleep.

"I'm sorry to be late. I worried you wouldn't wait. If you were not here, I would look for you on the beach tomorrow. You did consider not waiting, didn't you?"

"I wanted to have dinner with you, but if you didn't come, I would have thought of something else."

"Life's funny, isn't it? We plan, things change, we make new plans, and in the end, we don't know if what is, is better than what might have been. What would happen if we turned left versus right, did this rather than that? Or, in this case, if you did not wait for me? Can we ever be certain? I think so, but I can't say why. In any case, I'm glad you waited."

———

Shelly may have slept through the night had it not been for two women she would share the room with arriving two hours later.

"Shh, she's asleep. Let's put our stuff down and go eat. I'm starving," one whispered to the other as they entered the room, putting their suitcases near their beds.

As quietly as they tried to be, and because Shelly had slept for over two hours, she awoke, quickly sitting up.

"We're so sorry we woke you. We tried to be quiet. I'm Anne, this is my sister Susan, we're your roommates."

"I'm Shelly, and I'm glad you woke me. If you hadn't, I'd have woken up in the middle of the night hungrier than I am now."

Susan said, "Happy to meet you, Shelly. We're going out to get something to eat. Unless you have other plans, why don't you join us?"

"I don't want to intrude, but it would be nice to be with others tonight. If you're sure that's okay with both of you."

Anne quickly responded, "No bother, we'd love company other than just family." She said, smiling at her sister. "We just arrived, our first time here; we don't know where to go. Do you have any suggestions?"

Shelly thought for a moment before responding. Caribbean Paisano. She wasn't sure she was quite ready to share that memory with strangers.

I don't know where else to go. Other than sandwiches on the beach, that's the only other place Raymond and I were together.

"I do know one place that was reasonable with good food. Caribbean Paisano, Italian, a short walk from here. But I haven't been there in years, so no guarantee it will be as it was my first trip."

"You've been here before? How wonderful, we haven't. That place will be a good start, no matter how it turns out. And we want you to join us so we can pump you for more suggestions."

Where the three of them would have dinner decided, Shelly led Susan and Anne to the restaurant, and were quickly seated. Shelly was now happy she was not alone on this, her first time back in Caribbean Paisano. Everything looked exactly as she remembered. Bittersweet, but still, she was happy to be here. A conversation with Anne and Susan would be a good distraction from her memories of dinner here with Raymond.

"Thank you for joining us, Shelly. If you don't mind, we have many questions you might be able to answer."

"I'll try. What would you like to know?"

Anne spoke first.

"How long ago were you here? Were you alone or with someone else?"

This was not something Shelly wanted to talk about. She expected whatever she said would invite more questions about Raymond, she preferred not to answer.

"By myself. I came here as part of a year away from university trip. I'm from Zimbabwe in southern Africa."

"Zimbabwe! You're much further away from home than we are," Susan said. "How different are things now compared to them? What is there to do in and near St. John's?"

Shelly did her best to answer, never mentioning Raymond. She soon turned the conversation by asking Susan and Anne about themselves.

Dinner now over, the three of them split the check and headed back to the Antigua Inn. Susan and Anne were tired from their trip, especially after having wine with dinner. Shelly was more awake because she had napped before they arrived. Now in bed, she was left with her thoughts, trying to recall her dream. Slowly, it came back to her.

I was late meeting Raymond at Paisano. He waited. I told him I would have looked for him on the beach the next day had he not been there. The restaurant hasn't changed a bit, only the waiters, all of whom would have been too young to have worked there when Raymond and I were there.

Thinking about how much time had passed since her first trip to Antigua saddened Shelly. Little more than two kids trying to figure out the adult lives they were about to begin living. And now she's back, a middle-aged woman looking for...

I wish I knew.

CHAPTER
SIXTY-EIGHT

YOU INSISTED RAYMOND MEET YOU AND DON AT OTHER WORLDS COFFEE. *Why didn't you stay to meet him?*

I don't know; must there be a reason for everything?

Yes, but in many cases, this being one, we often don't want to acknowledge what is so obvious to others. You have visited a small number of the infinite, unlived lives you could have lived. You decided they were not what you wanted your immortal life to be. You had good reasons for not choosing them. *Do you for this last one?*

Good reasons? We're talking about how my soul will exist for eternity. You want me to pick one of the few lives I would have lived had I made different choices? You tell me to choose carefully. And now, for only the first time, you ask if I have good reasons for not choosing this one unlived life. What is it about whichever life I choose that is so special? Do you know something I don't?

I am you, Shelly, and you know all you need to know. The only difference is, I accept what you hide from yourself. You are choosing an eternal future for your immortal soul. I have told you to do so carefully. You know what you must do, but you haven't admitted to yourself what that is. Until you do, your soul will not rest. But there is one choice left for you to make.

Your search is incomplete. If you choose to continue visiting lives you would have lived had you made different choices in the past, you will find whatever would have come from those lives. If you choose not to do this, the choice will be made for you for all eternity. What do you choose?

I will continue.

CHAPTER
SIXTY-NINE

WAS IT WORTH THE TRIP? WOULD YOU DO IT AGAIN?

I'm not sure. I'm disappointed you weren't with me. However, I might be more disappointed had you been here.

Really? How so?

You have to know, Raymond. We are dead! We 'encounter' each other, but we are not together. What kind of relationship is that? And now in these crazy dreams I'm having. If this is to be our immortal "unlived lives," what is the point?

These dreams may lead us to something else. Something more real than our lives were before we died.

Do you honestly think so? I don't. We spent time together as kids in Antigua, and later, after the war, in Vietnam as young adults. We travelled together through Europe, ultimately to Zimbabwe, and you know how that ended. You also know, none of that happened. Asian made it clear that we were experiencing bits and pieces of lives we could have lived had we made different choices. None of that has changed.

I don't know what I know, but what if our eternity is all you just said? What do we do then? You are not happy, but you should consider how much worse things could have been. Shelly, wake up!

As though shaken by an unseen force, Shelly sat up in bed, seeing nothing in the dark room. She turned on the bedside lamp, looking around as though she expected someone to be there.

That was Raymond. I remember everything we said. He's reaching out to me. Does he know I am awake?

"Raymond, talk to me. I dreamed we were talking, it was too real not to be."

What would I do if he spoke to me? Ghosts don't talk; they keep people up at night. But I wasn't awake, I was asleep, dreaming. Every night I dream he is talking to me, and not about what has happened to each of us separately. We talk about us as a couple. Maybe he is right. We could be living our eternal lives. If so, at least we are together in some way.

———

And what if that is your eternal unlived life? Would that satisfy you?

It would have to if that's all there is.

Pay close attention to your dreams. What we say to each other in those dreams is important. These are not simply dreams, Shelly; they are the basis for the rest of our eternal lives.

ACKNOWLEDGMENTS

I thought I was done after writing Raymond Quinn's story. However, soon after publication, readers began asking about the next book. Who would be the main character? Would Raymond be in it? What did (insert character name) mean when they said (insert character's words)? People related to Raymond, Shelly, and all the other characters as I hoped they would.

So...I was *not* done.

Thinking about a sequel had me waking up at night mulling over storylines and losing countless hours of sleep. That wouldn't have happened had it not been for the thousands of readers who purchased *The Unlived Lives of Raymond Quinn*. Thank you all for your support, without which *The Unlived Lives of Shelly Bennett* never would have happened. (And, in spring 2026, look for *The Unlived Lives: Reckoning*.)

Now I look forward to your comments and questions about Shelly's journey through her unlived lives.

I also want to thank JT Farrell for his outstanding narration of Raymond's story. Many of those who listened to the story, told me that JT's voice brought my words to life. I created the characters, but it was you, JT, who gave them life. Thank you for that, I'm certain you have done the same for Shelly.

In 2013, I wrote and published *The 7 Keys to Change*, a book to help people better manage change at work and home. To be exact, I wrote it, and my good friend, Paula Johnson, handled the design and publishing. Paula is a master of many trades and a true creative as well. Thank you, Paula—my website designer, editor, marketing consultant, conscience, cover designer, and overall whip-cracker—for encouragement and suggestions, all balanced by carefully timed and deserved nagging.

You brought this project to completion, just as you did for *The 7 Keys* and *The Unlived Lives of Raymond Quinn*. Thanks for your support, not just for my books, but for your friendship, ideas, and hours of hard work on my behalf over the last four decades we've known each other.

DISCUSSION QUESTIONS

The best part about being in a book group is talking about what you've read. Here are a few questions to get you started.

1. Suicide is a trigger for many people who have considered it or have lost a loved one. Should suicide be avoided in fiction? If not, how should suicide be handled in fiction?
2. Shelly was deeply unhappy in Zimbabwe and was desperate to emigrate. What did her conduct in her unlived lives tell you about her personality?
3. Shelly makes connections and establishes relationships relatively quickly. How did this help or hinder her?
4. Which of your life's key decisions (education, job, partners, community, social circle, etc.) set you on a specific path?
5. If another version of your life is playing out—right now—in a parallel universe, where are you? What are you doing? What are your plans for the future? How is that 'you' different from you?

ABOUT THE AUTHOR

Like his Raymond Quinn character, William Matthies served in the U.S. Army, including a year-long stint in Vietnam with B Battery, 2nd Battalion, 19th Airborne Artillery, 1st Cavalry Division during the war. After the service, he graduated from college, married, raised two sons, and eventually found his true calling as a serial entrepreneur.

His most recent venture involved teaching the art and science of change management to organizations and individuals. His book, *The 7 Keys to Change*, is based on several years of research on how to manage both personal and professional change.

Pushing the envelope is second nature to Matthies. At 13, he and a friend embarked on a solo voyage to Catalina Island off the California coast. Their goal was a parent-free campout, but the result was a lifetime ban from the island.

That didn't stop him from visiting another island many years later, riding a bike from one end of Cuba to the other.

Matthies continues to seek out experiences to alter his perspective, including a Mach 2.5 flight in a MiG 25 supersonic Russian aircraft departing from Zhukovsky Air Base outside of Moscow.

He plays guitar in his spare time and has maintained absolute beginner status for more than three decades.

Matthies has yet to experience an alternate life while fully expecting to any day now.

www.ingramcontent.com/pod-product-compliance
Lightning Source LLC
Chambersburg PA
CBHW060310260626
47160CB00007B/2557